The Rev

Max Hennessy was the pen-name of John Harris. He had a wide variety of jobs from sailor to cartoonist and became a highly inventive, versatile writer. In addition to crime fiction, Hennessy was a master of the war novel and drew heavily on his experiences in both the navy and air force, serving in the Second World War. His novels reflect the reality of war mixed with a heavy dose of conflict and adventure.

Also by Max Hennessy

The Martin Falconer Thrillers

The Fledglings
The Professionals
The Victors
The Interceptors
The Revolutionaries

The RAF Trilogy

The Bright Blue Sky
The Challenging Heights
Once More the Hawks

The Captain Kelly Maguire Trilogy

The Lion at Sea
The Dangerous Years
Back to Battle

The Flying Ace Thrillers

The Mustering of the Hawks
The Mercenaries
The Courtney Entry

The REVOLUTIONARIES

JOHN HARRIS WRITING AS

MAX HENNESSY

CANELO

First published in the United Kingdom in 1978 by Hutchinson Junior Books

This edition published in the United Kingdom in 2022 by

Canelo
Unit 9, 5th Floor
Cargo Works, 1-2 Hatfields
London, SE1 9PG
United Kingdom

A CIP catalogue record for this book is available from the British Library.

Print ISBN 978 1 80032 847 1
Ebook ISBN 978 1 80032 082 6

Printed and bound in Great Britain by Clays Ltd, Elcograf S.p.A.

MIX
Paper from responsible sources
FSC® C018072
FSC www.fsc.org

Chapter 1

The old JN4 was painted like a circus and the engine clattered as if a large part of it were missing. A patch of undoped fabric rippled in the slipstream, the skeleton of the spars showing through, and one wing looked like a bandaged toe with the crude repairs that had been done on it. Along the fuselage behind me there were several tears, very roughly sewn up, which reminded me of my own earliest attempts to mend my first uniform.

But sky was sky and an aeroplane was an aeroplane; I hadn't been in the air since the autumn of the previous year and I'd been panting to get off the ground. Above me, the brilliant Texan sun shone through the fabric of the Jenny's upper wing, showing every spar and strengthener like the bat wings of a pterodactyl. There was a strong smell of petrol and hot oil around me, and the plane vibrated in a way that no well-tuned machine ought to behave. But I was incredibly, luxuriously happy, and the sound of the big Liberty engine crackling into life had filled me with a surging delight. Listening to it, head on one side, I had felt the machine quiver to my touch and as the propeller had whirled into invisibility and I had felt it flexing its muscles against the chocks – suddenly, under the thundering resonance, uneven though it was, something more alive than mere wood and steel could ever be, more vital than mere pounding pistons – I had felt alive again.

Now, peering over the side, I could see the flat plains of Texas beyond the foothills that ran up to the Sacramento Mountains and, on the other side, the length of the Edwards Plateau running down to the coastal plain and the swamps and bayous round Corpus Christi. Texas was a brutal land, harsh and cruel, and the people who lived in it – because they'd had to struggle with it through generations – were a tough people, resilient against disaster yet teak-hard when it came to endurance; for the most part big men, tall men made taller by the high-heeled boots they persisted in wearing, a relic of the days when men didn't fly aeroplanes and drive jalopies, but lived on horseback.

The Jenny had the look about her of that dreadful abortion, the BE12, which I'd flown in 1915 and 1916, with wide, double-strutted wings and a slender fuselage that looked too long for the engine. She was Curtiss-built, and was none the worse for that. When the Americans had come into the war in Europe in 1917, there had been only one aircraft factory in the United States worthy of the name – Curtiss; the rest were all small and incapable of fulfilling government contracts. And there had been only a handful of qualified aero engineers, though they'd made one great contribution to the victory in Europe, the Liberty engine, a big V-shaped motor that always seemed a lot better than the aeroplanes it pulled through the air.

I'd heard it had been designed in forty-eight hours in a hotel room in Washington, DC. It had originally been a 300-horse V8 but that hadn't been powerful enough and after redesign it had emerged as a 400-horse V12. Once they'd ironed out the bugs it had turned out to be a pretty good engine, which they'd pushed into British-designed de Havilland 4s, and the new American Jennies. Now, in the spring of 1920, so many had been sold as war surplus that everybody in the States who thought he was a flier had a DH or a Curtiss Jenny.

Most of them, however, took a bit more care of them than the owner of the one I was flying. He was a youngish man, clearly bitten as much by the bug of flying as I had been, but he was a great deal less experienced. He hadn't any idea of maintenance or the importance of servicing and I was careful not to move far away from the field so that if something went wrong I could get back in.

'I should be careful how you turn, old boy,' Slingsby had said as we swung into wind. 'The rudder or the aileron might fall off.' Since Slingsby was quite a flier himself, it wasn't bad advice.

Down below, they were selling hot dogs, and a band, hard straw hats on the back of their heads, their jackets discarded in the heat to show coloured sleeve bands, were pumping out a tune; a few people were sitting, nervously expectant, in horse-drawn buggies, gnawing on chicken bones and cold fried chops and letting the wrappings blow away in the breeze. There were a few motor cars on the edge of the field, too, containing hot little families eager to see something happen – the more dangerous the better, best of all if it was a fatal crash.

When the war had ended the United States War Department had demobilized thousands of pilots and sold at absurdly low prices thousands of the aeroplanes they'd been trained to fly; the two had come together as inevitably as iron filings to a magnet. But there were still no such things as government regulations, no inspection, no licensing of men or planes, and a pilot was just as good as he talked – and many were first-class orators. Skipping from town to town to put on displays and provide flights from farmers' fields, part aviators, part showmen, their little circuses were a peculiarly American institution. In Europe we'd been ready to move at the end of the war from combat to passenger flying, but in the vastness of the United States there was a great need to further air-mindedness in the country districts, and the best of these fliers did exactly that. The worst did just the opposite.

Either way, the age of the barnstormer had arrived in America.

Slingsby and I had arrived on the field merely as interested spectators but the itch to get into the air had been too much for us. They advertised a DH, a Jenny and an Avro. There was no sign of the DH and the Avro looked as if it might fall apart if started up, while the Jenny was only a little better, looking as if it had been rescued at the last minute from a scrapheap.

The owner, wearing a tight-fitting helmet with fluttering ribbons sewn to the crown, big bug-eyed goggles, a leather jacket, tight breeches and puttees, was with a man in a bowler hat attaching a notice to a fence – CLINT MATTHEWS WILL DEFINITELY HANG BY HIS TEETH BENEATH THE AEROPLANE.

'I hope they aren't false ones,' Slingsby said dryly. 'I can't imagine anything more nerve-wracking as you grip the rope between your jaws than seeing the old china snappers come out of your mouth.'

We didn't ask each other whether we'd like a trip. We just took it for granted, staring at the woebegone aeroplanes with a wistful longing, mixed with the sadness of professional pilots who saw what neglect had done to them.

Clint Matthews turned out to be a fraud. We came up behind him just as he was dishing out a long yarn about how he'd taken on Richthofen in his Jenny.

'That plane right there,' he was telling a farmer in bib overalls and a straw hat as he pointed to the battered aeroplane. 'August 1918. Over Château Thierry.'

We didn't bother to enlighten him but in August 1918 Richthofen had already been dead for four months, and if he hadn't he'd never been as far south as that; in any case Jennies hadn't flown much in Europe, and if they had they'd have been about as much use as a snowball in hell against Richthofen's Fokkers. We just told him we'd like a trip.

'Five dollars,' he said briskly. 'Take you up for five dollars.'

'We don't want taking up,' I said. 'We want to take her up ourselves.'

His jaw dropped. '*You* want to fly her?'

'Yes.'

'You can?'

'I'm sure we can.'

He laughed. 'Son, you need to have some flying hours in to take *that* crate up. Tricky things, Jennies.'

They were as placid as old mules, I knew, but I didn't argue in front of the farmer whose jaw was hanging open at the technicalities.

'I've got a few flying hours,' I said.

Matthews wasn't put off easily. 'I didn't take that thing up until I'd got at least fifty hours behind me,' he said. 'Now I've got a couple of hundred, I reckon I've just about got the know-how to handle her. How many hours you got, son?'

'A couple of thousand,' I said, 'give or take a few. Hard to say.'

'A couple of—' Matthews' jaw dropped '—who are you, bud? Richthofen?'

'No,' Slingsby said blandly. 'This is the chap who killed him.'

Matthews obviously believed him and his manner changed at once from boastfulness to obsequiousness. 'You Roy Brown? Gee, Mr Brown. I didn't recognize you there at first. I do now, of course.' He beamed. 'Hell, sure you can take her up! Ten dollars to you. How's that?'

We paid him the money and took off.

'You going to do some stunts?' he yelled as we moved off.

Not in that plane, we weren't. We just wanted to smell the sky and the dope and the hot oil again.

When we landed, Matthews appeared alongside us with a girl. She looked unbelievably young, but she wore breeches, helmet and leather jacket like Matthews himself.

'This is Mamie,' he said. 'My wife. She flies the Avro.' He grinned. 'When she'll start, that is. We are the Great Flying Circus. Sometimes she does a bit of wing-walking, and she flies the Jenny when I hang underneath by my teeth.' He grinned again. 'Ain't my teeth really, of course. I got a harness under my clothes and I clip it on but, from down here, it sure looks like I'm hanging on by the strap I've got in my mouth.'

His wife, a pale-faced waif of a girl, looked wretched. I had a feeling that she understood the age and decrepitude of the planes far more than Matthews and went through agony every time he left the ground.

'Sure expected more from you up there, Captain Brown,' Matthews said, 'with your reputation. A few stunts and so on.'

Since my name was Martin Falconer and I'd never met the man who'd killed Richthofen – though, oddly enough, I'd met Richthofen – I wasn't inclined to worry much what he thought of my reputation.

'Canadian, aren't you?' he said.

'No,' I said. 'English.'

'I thought you were Canadian.' He gestured. 'What in blazes are you doing down here in San José?'

Slingsby looked at me and I looked back at Slingsby. The same thought was going through both our heads. He might well ask. It was a good question. It had been a long pilgrimage for us and there weren't just the two of us. There were four. Four lost aviators escaped from the holocaust of the Civil War in Russia.

–

Under the Texas spring sunshine it was hard to remember just how awful it had been! We'd been sent to South Russia in 1919 by the British government to help the White Russian armies against the Bolsheviks who'd murdered the Tsar; but the muddle, the inefficiency of the Russian commanders, the unreliability of men who didn't enjoy fighting their compatriots, and finally the sudden switch of interest at home when Lloyd George had backed out of the affair, had resulted in the most appalling tragedy I'd ever seen in my young life, and left us high and dry in the middle of one of the most ghastly floods of refugees we'd ever seen. When I am an old man of eighty or ninety

– assuming I live that long, and since flying was still in its infancy, the chances were that I might not – I knew I'd still remember the Civil War in Russia. On my death bed, they'd find it engraved on my heart.

How 'Puddy' Pudhovkhin and 'Tommy' Tucker felt, I couldn't imagine, because Puddy had had a sister Olga, who had died of typhus on a hospital train. Puddy had found her body among the stiffening corpses of her patients and the hospital staff. Tommy's case was quite as bad. He'd been more than prepared to give his life to save Olga if necessary, and from the minute he'd met her, he'd had eyes for nobody else. But, in spite of everything, *he'd* survived, and so had I, and so had all the rest of us, even Puddy, and it had been shy, pretty, romantic little Olga who had died.

We'd been rescued from the Red Cavalry assault on Novorossiisk by the SS *Joseph Ellerman* entirely by chance: everybody else from the squadron was in the *SS Mercator*, headed for Batum to pick up more British servicemen who'd been stranded there, but in the scramble we four had found ourselves in an American ship. The captain, Cyrus K. Toynbee, had made it very plain that he'd had no intention of stopping anywhere before he reached the United States. Out of the kindness of his heart and with true American generosity, he'd taken his ship to Novorossiisk for no other reason than that he'd heard there were people there in need of help, but what he'd seen had shaken him to his foundations and he'd announced that, as far as he was concerned, he hoped he never saw 'Yurrup' again.

Until we'd learned of Olga's death and seen that last horrifying slaughter by the Red Cavalry, we'd all been cheering the idea of the States. My girl, Charley, happened to be in Mexico and I'd thought the chances of meeting her were suddenly very good. Tommy Tucker was glad because, being American, he'd decided to take his discharge from the RAF simply by discarding his uniform and walking away from it, knowing it would take a lot of doing to haul him back from the middle of his own countrymen. And Jimmy Slingsby, who was as mad as a hatter, had decided quite simply that it would be rather a lark to take a long leave from the RAF in the States, using Captain Toynbee's intransigence as an excuse.

With his normal overwhelming generosity Tommy was already concerned with making life bearable for Puddy, promising to find him a job in the States. 'The family's got a bit of the old cash,' he kept insisting. 'I'm sure we can find you something.'

Puddy's smile remained sad. He was a Russian: he simply couldn't imagine living so far from his beloved Russia. He'd lost everything – his home, his family, all his relations, every scrap of money his family had once owned – and Tommy's offer was a good one, but he wasn't yet able to absorb it. They were both badly in need of something to take their minds off Olga.

Slingsby and I had discussed having ourselves set ashore in Gib but, in the end, after Novorossiisk, we'd decided we too needed a change from a Europe that was already beginning to suffer all the depressions of the post-war scene. It hadn't been hard to persuade Captain Toynbee to back us up. The only precaution I took was to slip ashore when we went alongside in Lisbon to coal ship, and send off a couple of hurried cables. One went to Ludo Sykes, my commanding officer, who was doubtless at that moment waiting for me to turn up somewhere in the Middle East. It stated laconically that, thanks to Captain Toynbee and the possibility of typhus aboard his ship, we weren't allowed ashore, and that as a result we were requesting permission to take a little disembarkation leave in the States when we arrived. The other was to Ludo's cousin Charley, my girl, who was in Veracruz, where her father had landed a job with the Cowdray petrol company, Mexican Eagle. I gave her Tommy's home address in San José, Texas, and suggested she meet me there. If that didn't get her on a ship to New Orleans, nothing would.

When we arrived, New Orleans was like the hobs of hell, and different from anything I'd ever seen before. Hot and humid in the same way as Batum, its French–Spanish background was clearly visible and it seemed to be full of wrought-iron balconies and the smell of oleander. Tommy explained that it lay so low it was below the level of the Mississippi at high tide and had to be protected by high embankments called levees. He showed us round the cemeteries where, because of the water-saturated soil, bodies were buried in vaults often twelve feet above ground level.

Because of the new prohibition laws it was impossible to buy a drink openly, but Tommy left us sitting in the park while he went to see a solicitor he knew who acted occasionally for his family. He came back with a roll of dollars with which he paid for the civilian trousers and shirts we bought, and the name of a man who would sell us a carton of beer. The bootlegger had a dark office behind a saloon that looked like something out of a Wild West film, and although the notice on the swing doors said the place sold only soft drinks, in the room at the back there were four round tables and, with a great deal of winking, nodding and conspiratorial whispering, we ended up with a couple of bottles of beer each. It seemed a funny way of having a drink.

'Prohibition don't seem to prohibit much,' Slingsby observed.

'I guess they soon learned the way round it,' Tommy grinned. 'What we drink these days comes from the West Indies, Cuba, Bermuda, Canada and places like that, but you're best to stick to beer, because some of the so-called whisky's home-made from wood alcohol and can send you blind, and the gin's usually made in the bath-tub. They say it fetches the paint off the bath-tub and the enamel off your teeth.'

I'd never seen so many motor cars in my life. There were Chevrolets, Franklins, Fords, Stutzes and a dozen other makes I'd never even heard of: sedans, limousines, roadsters and coupés, all high and heavy and equipped with vast yellow lights like glowing eyes, all clattering and roaring and backfiring so that the streets were blue with smoke and acrid with the smell of burnt petrol.

'The motoring craze has sorta caught on over here,' Tommy explained.

For the fun of it we took a horse-cab to the station, where Tommy paid our fares to San José. I tried to give him an IOU but he refused.

'My folks aren't exactly without the old dollars,' he pointed out.

At San José, after passing through the foothills of the mountains, we climbed down from the train at a small station and found a big Franklin waiting for us in the dusty square beyond the wooden railway buildings. We'd expected the Tucker home to be a good-size ranch, because Tommy was clearly not short of money; it turned out to be palatial. Built in the Mexican style, it was a low *adobe* building which included the family's lavish suites, the office, the commissary, kitchens and the *mayor-domo*'s comfortable quarters, while in the opposite wing were the stables, smithy, workshops, barns and waggon sheds, and the quarters of the house servants, stable boys and the cattle hands, several of them – because they were close to the border – Mexicans who'd sought work in the States.

Tommy's father, known to everybody as Big Dan, was a giant of a man, sixty-odd with long legs and bowed shoulders. Mrs Tucker was dead but the house was run by Tommy's sister Evaline, whom he'd obviously briefed by cable from the lawyer's office in New Orleans, because she immediately grabbed hold of Puddy and started to make him feel at home. Since Puddy was one of the best types of Russian aristocrats, tall, good-looking, well-mannered and with a nice sense of humour when he was in a state to let it show, she seemed to get as much pleasure out of it as Puddy did.

Charley hadn't let us down and there was a long cable which must have cost her a fortune to say she'd meet us at El Paso on 18 May. She'd be staying, she announced, at the Paso del Norte Hotel, and she'd have with her a friend who'd accompanied her through Mexico by train because she was heading for Los Angeles.

'Not one girl,' Slingsby said delightedly. 'But *two*!'

'As far as you're concerned,' I told him firmly, 'one! Charley's mine.' I turned to Tommy. 'But why El Paso? Why not New Orleans?'

Tommy shrugged. 'Well, we closed the border in 1916, but I guess mebbe they've opened it again now the revolution's almost over.'

Slingsby's eyebrows shot up. 'You've got a revolution over here, too?' he said.

Tommy grinned. 'You must have read about it in the London papers.'

'We've been rather busy. If you remember, there was a bit of a war goin' on over there.'

Tommy's smile grew wider. 'There's been a bit of a war going on over here, too. In Mexico. There's been a revolution taking place ever since 1910 when Madero overthrew Don Porfirio Díaz.'

'Don Porfirio who?'

'Díaz. He inherited Mexico from Juárez who threw out Maximilian of Austria when he tried to make himself Emperor in the eighteen-sixties. After Maximilian was shot Juárez took over, and Díaz took over from Juárez; Madero took over from Díaz and Huerta took over when Madero was shot. Venustiano Carranza took over from Huerta but he's on his way out too now, so it'll be Alvaro Obregón by this time, I guess.'

We stared at each other, wondering just what we were letting ourselves in for. Tommy's smile widened. 'It's all over,' he promised. 'Honest! Díaz, Huerta and Carranza were just dictators. Obregón's sworn there'll be a democratic government. They say he'll buy off Villa.'

'Who's Villa?'

'Pancho Villa. He supported Madero but he didn't like Huerta and Carranza. Come to that, Obregón neither. I guess the only guy Pancho Villa really has much time for is Pancho Villa himself. He's actually only a bandido but he sure knew how to fight wars. The *peóns* liked him because he smashed the Spanish overlords. He was a mixture of Robin Hood, Attila the Hun and Jesse James, I guess, all well-flavoured with red-hot chilli sauce. At times he actually did rob the rich to feed the poor, but I guess he also had a short temper and a liking for cruelty. You could say he was the symbol of the savagery and confusion of the times.'

Three days later a letter arrived from Charley. The troubles in Mexico, she said, seemed to be over, and they'd been told it was safe to travel via Mexico City. There appeared to be no government, because, as Tommy had suggested, the latest president, Carranza, had just been chased out of office by the new man, Obregón; but the place was calm and she rather fancied having a look round a city which had been so greatly in the news instead of travelling by sea. She was well in control, it seemed, and didn't intend to miss any fun there was going.

By this time, thanks largely to Tommy and Tommy's family, Puddy was looking more alive. For Puddy nothing could have been better than a visit to the States. Dan Tucker lent him a horse, and he and Tommy went off for a whole day at a time, sometimes alone, sometimes with Tommy's sister Evalina, who clearly suddenly had eyes for nobody but Puddy. Slingsby and I were definitely out of it. Perhaps they'd decided that, since we'd been looking after ourselves throughout the war from 1914 to 1918, we could cope without much effort on their part.

Because there were stacks of magazines and books about the house, in the two or three days they left us alone I learned a great deal about what had been going on south of what they all called the Tex–Mex border. What Tommy had said was right. There *had* been a bit of a war going on and a horrifying story it was, too – of cold-blooded, cynical political adventurers seizing power one after the other, not for the good of the country but purely for personal gain. As a history of anarchy, bloodshed and witless savagery, it was beaten by the civil war in Russia solely by its size.

But sitting around reading suited neither Slingsby nor me and one day, when the three of them had gone off once more, Slingsby and I, who'd heard of the fliers who'd arrived nearby, had gone to pay homage once more to the everlasting aeroplane and sniff in a few lungfuls of dope and hot oil.

Which, in effect, was the answer to Clint Matthews' question – what were we doing in San José? – and explained why we'd been flying an ancient Jenny that looked about to fall apart at the seams.

–

Matthews was pulling his helmet down now and adjusting his goggles. The air war in Europe had already arrived in the American pulp magazines and they were churning out the stories in hundreds – mostly written by men who'd never been off the ground – wildly extravagant and usually attributing the victory to the American Air Force which, in fact, hadn't really got going until late 1918. No word was ever written about people like Tommy Tucker.

Matthews obviously tried to live up to the image. In his tight breeches, the yellow scarf he allowed to flutter behind him, and the ribbons on his leather cap, he looked just like one of the illustrations from *Aces High* or *Death in the Air.*

'Guess I'll go and give the folks their show,' he said. 'Give 'em a few fierce stunts and so on.'

'In that?' Slingsby breathed as he turned to the Jenny.

'Finest bus ever flew on the Western Front,' Matthews said as he walked away.

Slingsby pulled a face. And no wonder. The Jenny's wheels, which were uncapped, looked like something off a bicycle, and the coffin-shaped fuselage, encased in best nitrate-doped Irish linen, shuddered as if it had the shakes.

'Made outa the tail assembly of one, the wings of a second and the engine of a third.' The words came in a growl from a small leathery individual in a flat cap like a frying pan, a stiff celluloid collar that was worn at the edges and had gone black, and a pullover knitted in alternate stripes of red, yellow, green and blue so he looked a little like a wasp.

'This is Red,' Mrs Matthews said, introducing him. 'He's the mechanic. He looks after things.'

'When we got the money,' Red pointed out. 'Which ain't often. That—' he cocked a thumb at the

Jenny that Matthews was climbing into '—she shakes like she got the ague and she ain't nothing else but a butter churn with wings.'

Whistling 'She Wore A Yellow Ribbon', Matthews was settling himself in the cockpit now and Red gave him a sour look. 'Ain't never exactly the thing for flying in the sort of weather you get down here,' he said. 'We once had the engine cowling blow off and wreck the stabilizer, and the first one we lost was because a vertical air current slammed her down and left her stranded in a tree.'

Looking at the Jenny, I could well believe him.

'Any mountain over five thousand feet's too high to fly over,' he went on gloomily. 'So you gotta go between 'em down the canyons. And, brother, you sure gotta be careful the one you choose don't come to a dead end. The sand plays hell with the engines and the dry climate warps the propellers, and most of the carburettors are defective anyway, like the magnetos, and the manifolds are always condensing moisture which gets into the carburettor and stops the engine cold.' He lit a cigarette and blew out smoke. 'She's out of true, does ninety miles an hour flat out and, if we could afford to, we'd throw her away and buy another. But we can't, and she sure is hell on wheels to fly.'

By this time, watched by the gaping crowd, Matthews was adjusting his scarf and helmet ribbons, making sure they gave the true romantic picture of a daredevil ace, and I noticed he spent more time on that than he did on checking the aircraft, because he'd not bothered to look at the tyres or the control surfaces or even the fuselage.

His wife was staring after him with huge frightened eyes. 'I sure wish he'd go back to the hardware store,' she said quietly. 'He had a good job in the hardware store.'

Matthews needed someone to tell him he was acting like an idiot, but he'd never have believed them so it wouldn't have done much good. He'd survived so far, I guessed, by sheer luck, and had come to believe it was experience.

As the Jenny started up, Slingsby's face grew bleak. James Alonzo St John Slingsby had a reputation for being mad but the madness was tempered by sheer experience. When Slingsby trailed a wing a foot above the ground as he came in to land, it was because he knew he could do it and his aeroplane wouldn't let him down. He was a languid young man, pale to the point of anonymity, with pale hair, pale eyes and pale skin. But there'd never been anything pale about his flying or his nerves, despite the innocent expression he wore, and, though his chief claim to fame was an enormous appetite that never seemed to put a pound on his slim frame, in fact he was a first-rate pilot. He was watching Matthews now as he swung the Jenny round, showing off again before the crowd and the man he thought had killed Richthofen.

'I think I'd like to leave,' he said quietly. 'I'm not going to enjoy this.'

We climbed into the Franklin Tommy had loaned us and chugged across the field. By this time the Jenny was about a thousand feet up, doing tight turns to the awed gasps from the crowd. Matthews's wife was still watching, and I noticed as we passed that her hands were clenched at her sides and she was standing as stiff as a statue, as if she felt that any movement on her part might upset the delicate balance of the battered machine just turning over our heads.

'I hope he doesn't try a loop,' I said.

'He's barmy enough,' Slingsby decided.

We tried hard to forget Matthews but, as we swung towards the gate and the dusty road towards San José, above the clatter of the Franklin's engine we heard the battered Liberty cough. As I heaved on the handbrake and the Franklin slid to a stop across the grass with the wheels locked, we swung round in our seats and stared upwards. Matthews's wife had her clenched fists to her mouth now and the old farmer in the bib overalls stood behind her, his heavy gnarled hands hanging by his side, his eyes on the plane, his face devoid of expression.

The Jenny had been making a steep climb but now, with the maltreated engine coughing and totally without power or flying speed, the nose had dropped into a stall and the wings turned into a flicking nose-down twist.

'Oh, my God!' Slingsby said.

I knew without being told that Matthews's experience didn't extend to recovering from a spin, certainly not at a thousand feet up.

'Cross your controls—' Slingsby was kneeling up on the seat '—cross your controls, man!'

But whatever Matthews was doing up there it was making no difference to the Jenny. She was hurtling earthwards like a plummet now, her wings catching the sunshine as she twisted her way down. As we watched, something broke loose and fluttered away. It looked like an aileron and after it came a few more fragments. The ill-treated, unserviced plane was breaking up in the air; if we'd treated it as Matthews had treated it, it would probably have done the same to us.

A thick groaning sound escaped the old farmer. Mamie Matthews's hands opened and covered her face and a thin wailing sound came from her throat, hoarse and terrified like a frightened animal's cry.

At the last moment the plane seemed to level off – as though by some miracle Matthews had done the right thing – and the dive became less steep. But the undercarriage caught the top of a barn and we saw tiles fly upwards in a shower as the Jenny vanished from sight beyond the pecan trees. A wheel shot high into the air, with a few scraps of wreckage to show the force of the crash, then we saw a puff of smoke and a flare of flame, and the whole sky beyond the barn began to shimmer in the rising column of smoke from the appalling sudden heat generated by a petrol blaze.

Red, the mechanic, had put one arm round Mamie Matthews's shoulder and I saw her whole frame hunched up and shaking with terrible sobs. As women ran towards her, Slingsby sighed.

'Shouldn't think there's much we can do,' he said.

I put the Franklin into gear and turned on to the dust road. Everybody was running across the field now, their eyes starting out of their heads, eager as ghouls to see the disaster. Leading the stampede was a black Ford tourer and a buggy on which a man was whipping its two horses to a frenzied gallop.

'Chaps like that,' Slingsby observed, 'are putting aviation back twenty years.'

Chapter 2

When we reached the Tucker ranch Tommy and the others were back.

Tommy listened to the story of the crash with a grave face.

'The wonder is that more of 'em aren't killed,' he said. 'They get aviation a bad name, because everybody associates flying with death, and all they do is kill themselves and their passengers. They fly off fields that aren't big enough and give joyrides to people who panic. When the fabric of their machines tear, they mend the hole with a piece from their shirts, and when a strut goes, they bind it with baling wire. It isn't much of a life, I guess, but they don't know anything about flying, and when they kill themselves – which they often do – all they get is a ride under a stained tarpaulin to the back door of a village store somewhere out in the sticks, and a screwed-down coffin hurriedly made by a local carpenter.'

'Aviators' coffins are always hurriedly made,' Slingsby said dryly. 'And they're always screwed down so the relatives can't see inside.'

Over dinner that night, the crash came up again.

'What are you boys going to do now you've finished flying?' Tommy's father asked.

'I've not finished flying,' Tommy said.

'You won't find much opportunity for flying round here, son.'

'Why not?' Tommy gestured. 'The world's become flying-conscious since the war. In a few years from now, people will be flying all over the States. They'll be carrying mail in aeroplanes and the trains'll be empty.'

Dan Tucker laughed. 'Don't give me that,' he said.

Tommy leaned forward. 'People will be flying the Atlantic, Pa,' he said earnestly. 'The transatlantic liners will be empty.'

'You sure have some imagination, son.'

'They've already flown non-stop from Newfoundland to Ireland,' I pointed out.

'That isn't New York to Paris, and Americans won't want to travel from New York to Newfoundland and then from Ireland to Paris. They won't have gained a thing.'

'Ten years from now,' I said, 'they'll fly direct from New York to Paris or London. With passengers.'

'In those flimsy things?'

'They won't always be flimsy, Mr Tucker. And they're developing better motors every year.'

'Won't help much round here,' Evalina said to Tommy. 'And I thought you were coming back to help run the ranch.'

Tommy thumped the table. 'Say, there's an idea, Puddy,' he grinned. 'I've got a job for you.'

'Where?'

'Here.'

Puddy's handsome face turned quickly to Evalina and then back again. He was holding a cigarette in the back-to-front fashion all Russians used, which seemed to fascinate her. 'What do I do?' he asked.

'We're aviators,' Tommy announced. 'Let's aviate. I reckon we can save days rounding up cattle if we have an aeroplane to find 'em first. We'll buy one and you can maintain it and use it to fly Pa down to the ranch in San Martino when he wants to go.'

'You've got a ranch in San Martino, too?' Slingsby said.

'Yeah.' Tommy smiled. 'One in Marion, too. And a hardware business in Houston. It'll be useful to be able to visit 'em so easily. After all, over the plains the weather's usually good for flying and there's plenty of ground to land on.'

Tommy's enthusiasm was infectious and Evalina clapped her hands. His father looked alarmed, however.

'Hey, wait a minute, you guys!' he said. 'Who says we need an aeroplane?'

Tommy leaned forward. 'How long does it take you to find your steers when you lose 'em in the *arroyos*.'

'Few days. That's all.'

'You could find 'em in an hour in an aeroplane and send your men direct to them. Save two men three days' work.'

The old man looked startled.

'In winter, you could drop bales of hay to stranded cattle. In summer you could search out the water holes that aren't dried out. You could pick up a vet in San José for a sick steer and have him alongside it in an hour.'

The old man looked impressed, but he was too old to give way easily.

'You cain't teach an old dog new tricks, son,' he said.

'A few *rancheros* are already using automobiles,' Tommy went on eagerly. 'Eventually, they'll use aeroplanes. You could get down to San Martino or Marion in an hour. You could drop in unexpectedly at Houston and make sure things are okay there. Last year that manager you had was swindling you, and it took you two years to find out because he always knew when you were coming. With an aeroplane you could be there in an hour. Aeroplanes are the future.'

Slingsby grinned. 'And then some,' he said.

The following morning Charley and her friend were due in El Paso, so we got up early and were driven down to San José in the Franklin. It was as big as a liner, and even with five of us in it we bounced around like peas in an empty pod. There was plenty of room for two girls but the dust was terrible. The *mesquite*, the cactus and the pecan trees were yellow with it, and it got into your hair and eyes and up your nostrils.

'They say Texas has more of everything than anywhere else,' Tommy grinned. 'It sure has more dust, that's for certain.'

We caught the train at San José, a long line of coaches pulled by a huge engine with a cowcatcher at the front and a thing like a tea-kettle on the funnel that reminded me of the trains in Russia. The service was a lot more efficient, though, and we not only left on time but arrived in El Paso without a hitch.

The town was full of soldiers on leave, dozens of young men in khaki staring round them with open mouths.

'National Guards,' Tommy said. 'Bit like English Territorials. I guess everybody's still a bit scared of Villa.'

'Where is he now?'

'Not far away, I bet.' Tommy gestured across the river, where we could see the Mexican town of Ciudad Juárez beyond the International Bridge. 'He tangled with the States in June, last year. He had a go at Juárez and bullets came across the border, killed a guy and wounded several others. They sent the Seventh Cavalry after him and his men were scattered. He got away but his army was smashed.'

Slingsby looked interested. 'Does he do that sort of thing often?'

'Sure does. He raided Columbus just to the east of here in 1916. They arrived in the middle of the night, yelling '*Viva Villa*', killed a few soldiers and civilians and lifted a lot of rifles. The United States Government sent a punitive expedition after him, under General Pershing.'

'Into Mexico?'

'Wasn't the first time. We had to occupy Veracruz in the south for a while in Huerta's time, and when Villa raided Columbus they didn't hesitate.' He grinned. 'I guess the punitive expedition didn't do such a lot of punishing because they never found him. But at least they did scatter him all over Chihuahua and it did show what a mess we'd let the army get into. They'd just pulled it together when we entered the war in Europe in 1917.'

'Rehearsal sort of thing?' Slingsby said.

'Well they used lorries and motor cars for the first time. But about the only worthwhile things that happened were the cavalry charge at Ojos Azules, and a guy called Georgie Patton who was attacked by three *bandidos* and shot the lot and brought them back draped across the front of his car like they were bucks he'd killed. It was the expedition that got Pershing command of the American Army in Europe. By then he was the only American general who'd had any experience of war since Cuba at the turn of the century. And even that wasn't so very much.'

'And what about now?' I asked – in some alarm, because I didn't quite see Charley taking particularly kindly to having her progress arrested by a set of bandits. She belonged to one of the oldest families in England, and I had a feeling I could offer odds on her winning every time in a confrontation with a Mexican bandit.

Tommy smiled. 'Nothing to worry about,' he said. 'He's not been very active since the Seventh Cavalry chased him out of Juárez. He's had ten years of fighting and they say he wants to retire.'

El Paso was a dusty town built round the railway. Here and there were portly business blocks but there were still a lot of *adobe* and wooden buildings with *ramadas* outside where horses were tied; though it looked vaguely Mexican, it was still solidly American with ice-cream parlours and what had been saloons until prohibition had put paid to them.

Tommy kept up a running commentary about what had happened there, and how Wesley Hardin, the gunfighter, had been in and out of the town more than once before he was shot.

'When the Mex revolution was in full swing,' he explained, 'everybody used to come down here and sit on the roofs to watch the fighting between the Maderistas and Porfirio Díaz's troops. The housewives used to give battle parties and invite their friends up and serve 'em coffee and lend 'em binoculars to see the fun. I watched it once before I went to Canada to join the RAF. It all came to a stop when a few machine-gun bullets came across the border and we all had to dive for cover.'

The main streets were asphalted and lined with gift shops selling diamond rings made of glass, and Navajo blankets and trinkets which Tommy said had come from Chicago.

'Americans always have one eye open for a fast buck,' he pointed out.

Postcards of Villistas riddled with bullets were selling like hot cakes, grisly souvenirs which Tommy said the National Guardsmen – most of whom had still to hear a shot fired in anger – bought to send home to their families and girl friends to indicate what a dangerous life they were living.

We saw the plaque on the wall of the boarding house where Wesley Hardin had been shot – I couldn't quite see them putting up a plaque in England to Crippen or Charley Peace – and visited the well-guarded International Bridge across the Rio Grande which formed the Tex–Mex border. The town on the other side looked as though it had been through a mincing machine. The bullring had been burned, together with the customs house, the railway station and a hardware store, and there were bullet holes in every wall.

'Villa's machine-gunners,' Tommy explained.

We could see weapons everywhere and those Mexicans who were not sleeping in the sun under their enormous sombreros seemed to be riding bony ponies, stooping under the weight of the weapons and ammunition they wore.

Eventually we wandered back to the station. After a while it occurred to us that there was no sign of any train arriving at the other side of the river.

'Won't be no train,' the elderly station clerk explained.

'What!' Tommy's yell could be heard all down the platform. 'Why not?'

'That guy Guzmán's out on the rampage!'

'Who's Guzmán?' I asked.

Tommy grinned. 'Esplenderoso Benavenides Guzmán,' he said. 'Known on this side of the border as Splendid Ben or Gorgeous Gus. He rather likes it, I've heard, and dresses the part. *Charro* costume with gold coins on his sombrero, and silver filigree on his saddle. On the other side he's known as Escatimoso Guzmán, which means Cunning Guzmán. He was in the Villa raid on Columbus, and he doesn't like Americans because one of them shot his brother at Ojos Azules.'

The clerk was nodding.

'Sure don't,' he agreed. 'He was one of Villa's Dorados.'

In their enthusiasm they seemed to have forgotten the point.

'And what the hell has this bloody Splendid Ben done to the train?' I asked.

The clerk jumped and turned. 'Ain't done nothing to the train, Mister,' he said. 'He just pulled up the track north of Chihuahua City, that's all. They've sent a bus to meet the passengers. That'll sure be a ride.' The old man cackled. 'Them Mex roads ain't like ours.'

I could imagine what Charley would have to say. Doubtless it would be in the voice she used on unwanted young men who tried to make dates with her.

'Good job there ain't many passengers ever,' the clerk went on. 'The revolution cut the numbers some. Usually only a dozen or two these days.'

Tommy shrugged and turned to me. 'It looks as though we'd better get something to eat,' he said. 'And come back later when they arrive.'

'That won't do no good neither,' the clerk said.

Tommy whirled. 'Why not?'

'Ain't coming here.' The clerk seemed to think it all a great joke.

'Not coming here?' Tommy's voice deepened. 'Where the blazes are they going then?'

'Camarillo. Down towards Presidio and Ojinaga. It's nearer. Over the mountains. Reckon they'll be almost there now.'

Tommy swore. 'Come on,' he said. 'I guess we'd better hire a car or something.'

We found a garage where they had a big Stutz for hire and we all crammed into it. Pulling the hand brake firmly on, Tommy set the spark and the throttle levers and pulled the choke out.

'Okay,' he said. 'Crank her.'

Slingsby heaved on the handle and the Stutz started up with a screech and a roar, filling the yard with blue smoke until Tommy adjusted the throttle and the choke, then the engine slowed to a clatter that would have done no more than waken the dead.

'All aboard,' Tommy yelled. 'I guess the girls'll be at the hotel there by now and trying to telephone my Old Man.'

The Stutz was an enormous car with huge headlamps built for acetylene gas but converted to electricity, a klaxon horn, nickel-plated hubcaps and rubber-cushioned pedals. By the standards of 1920 it was supposed to be hell on wheels as a motor car, but it was still like riding in a tank. The road was dreadful and the dust was enough to choke you, but we roared along as fast as Tommy could drive, a great yellow cloud hanging in the air behind us.

'Do we bring 'em back in this?' I yelled above the din.

'Guess so.'

'I reckon you'd better send a cable to Evalina to have a bath ready,' Slingsby said.

It was much later than we expected when we first saw the lights of Camarillo. By the number of them, it wasn't a very big town. The road wound down a long hillside where the going was rough and, though Tommy terrified the life out of us with the speed, it was still after midnight before we reached the outskirts.

It was the usual small-town border huddle of *adobe* and wood buildings, flat-faced and ugly. There were still a few lights on and from somewhere the sound of a guitar being played softly.

'Quietened down a bit since prohibition,' Tommy observed. 'Used to be jumping in the old days, like all the other border towns. I guess they buy their booze from across the river these days and take it home to drink in the back parlour.'

He had no idea where the hotel was and decided we'd better stop to enquire. I could imagine Charley stretched out on a bench in the saloon by this time, wondering when someone was coming to rescue her. We climbed out of the car to stretch our legs while Tommy, who spoke Spanish with the Mexican hands on his father's ranch, decided to look for someone to ask.

There was a walloping great moon, almost full and looking like a huge medallion in the sky, and you could see the trees throwing enormous black shadows over the dusty road which looked as if it had been painted with silver lacquer. A guitar was twanging softly and someone was singing a cynical Mexican ditty in English –

'If to my window comes Porfirio Díaz
Give him for charity cold tortillas,
If to my window comes General Huerta
Spit in his face and slam the door—'

It seemed to go on for ages, naming every one of the would-be dictators who'd plagued the history of Mexico ever since the end of the last century.

As Tommy disappeared, we sat down on the boardwalk, tired, sweaty, dusty, all of us with thirsts like camels, and wondering if we could get a couple of rooms at the hotel – when we found it – because we didn't particularly feel like driving all the way back that night. I had a strong suspicion that the hotel would already be full of people from the delayed train and I wasn't looking forward to sleeping on the floor, Charley or no Charley.

I was just about to say so, in fact, when I heard the sound of horses' hooves. They came suddenly, from silence, as though the horses had been kicked from a standstill into a full gallop, then there was a crackle of shots that brought us all to our feet. The song stopped abruptly and, just as we were wondering what the hell was going on, Tommy appeared at a flat run.

'Get under cover,' he yelled. 'Get under cover! It's Villa!'

As we started running, I heard high-pitched yells which I could just make out as '*Viva Guzmán*' and '*Tierra y libertad*' and a few other things I didn't understand, then round the corner and down the street from the direction of the border poured a river of horsemen, all screaming and shooting and yelling. The ground shook under the flying hooves and, as we dived over a row of barrels and threw ourselves flat behind them, they thundered past like the Charge of the Light Brigade. Bullets whacked into woodwork and gouged chunks out of the *adobe* buildings behind us, and I heard glass shatter and a few shrieks – then they were gone.

'I thought you said the revolution was over!' I snorted.

Tommy grinned sheepishly. 'It's supposed to be.'

'Well, it doesn't seem to be over here. Who are they?'

'They sounded like Splendid Ben's boys, not Villa's.'

I lifted my head. Down the street it sounded as though a riot was in progress. 'Hadn't we better investigate?' I suggested.

'It'll soon be over,' Tommy said. 'It happens from time to time. They drink too much *tequila* and splash across the Rio Grande, then go like the blazes through the town, shooting a few windows out, and out at the other side.'

'It seems to be a bit more than that this time,' I said.

Tommy frowned. 'Since you mention it,' he said, 'it does. Perhaps we ought to join in.'

We climbed back into the Stutz and, cranking it up, headed into the town. In the distance we could see the sky lit by flames and a few horsemen milling around in the middle of the square. As we passed the end of a dark unlit street, I heard hooves again and the next second we seemed to be surrounded by terrified steers being stampeded to the river. A couple of horsemen thundered past firing rifles and whacking at the steers with their big sombreros. Spotting us, one of them fired at us and missed, but it seemed to me I was staring right down the barrel because the flame of the shot seemed to fill my eyes. A third horseman some distance behind them almost hit the car in the dark. At the last minute he tried to swerve but the horse's feet slid away from it in the dust, and it skittered, lost its balance and went down alongside the car with a crash. The rider went across the street rolled up like a ball and crashed into the wheel of a parked cart. He made no attempt to move and I jumped from the car and ran towards him, picking up a loaded Mondragón rifle he'd dropped on the way. The Mexican seemed to be either dead or unconscious because he didn't move as I bent over him, but then he suddenly came to life and I saw a knife glint in the moonlight. Without thinking, I hit him as hard as I could under the jaw with the butt of the Mondragón and he went over on to his back, and this time he really did seem to be out.

I took the knife from his fingers and threw it away, then stripped him of his weapons. He had another rifle and two revolvers and enough ammunition in the belts slung round his body to sink a battleship. He stank like a polecat of sweat and dirt and cheap wine. Tommy's guess that the raiders, whoever they were, had been nursing their resentment against the Americans in a *cantina* at the other side of the river until some chance word had sent them off in a drunken charge to lash out at the hated *Yanquis* seemed to be about right.

I tossed the revolvers and rifles to the others, and we all felt much better with weapons in our fists. Seeing two of the bandits passing in front of the flames, dragging an old woman after them, Tommy picked them off one after the other, and the old lady, who probably wasn't as old as she looked, took to her heels in the opposite direction. From the two bodies we retrieved two more rifles and two more revolvers, which we tossed into the car.

There was quite a bit of shooting going on now and some of the shots were coming our way.

'I reckon if we're not careful,' I pointed out, 'somebody's going to think we belong to Splendid Ben. Don't you think we ought to get inside somewhere?'

It was my idea to work my way through back doors and back gardens down the street towards the hotel. By this time, I imagined Charley would be wondering where we'd got to and when I was going to turn up to fish her out of this unholy stew that had brewed up so suddenly. Unless, of course, using her training as a nurse, she was on her knees somewhere beside some wounded man, or – being a Bartelott-Diveton-Sykes, never a family to allow themselves to be pushed around – was behind a Mondragón or a Winchester, taking a potshot or two herself.

We pushed open a door and fell inside a darkened house.

'Who's there?' A hoarse voice came out of the darkness.

'Don't worry,' Tommy said. 'We're Americans.' He paused. 'Leastways,' he added, 'some of us are.'

'Where are them dratted Mexes?' A light came on and a thin stringy man wearing trousers and a woollen vest appeared, holding a rifle. Behind him was a woman with a coat thrown over her nightdress, and two frightened children.

'Dratted *bandidos*,' the man said. 'Always at it! A body cain't live in peace nohow!'

There was still a lot of noise nearer the centre of the town but it had grown more quiet where we were, so we crept out of the back door, over a fence and down an alley. As we emerged at the end of it, a horseman came thundering towards us. Acting on the understanding that anybody on a horse was an enemy, Slingsby reversed his Mondragón and, as the Mexican came past, swung it with all his strength. The butt caught the Mexican full in the face and broke off at the butt; the Mexican went over the tail of the horse as if he were shot.

'Four,' Puddy said.

We picked up another rifle and two more revolvers.

'Gettin' quite an armoury,' Slingsby said. 'We could make a fortune sellin' 'em when the war's over.'

We left the Mexican groaning in the shadows and moved on again. We had almost reached the plaza now. The flames lit up the whole place and we could see horsemen galloping backwards and forwards. Pushing out of a lane between two houses, we ran full into a Mexican who fired at me at point-blank range. The blast seared my face and the bullet lifted my hat off, but Puddy shot him dead in his tracks, and we sprinted across the plaza looking for the hotel and some corner where we could use our rifles.

There seemed to be utter confusion. A few American voices were yelling above the din.

'Where's the sheriff? Tell that guy to break out some guns!'

'The damn guns are locked up and the sheriff's disappeared!'

'So where's his deputy?'

A few panic-stricken inhabitants had locked themselves in an *adobe* building; we hammered on the door and yelled to them to let us in, but they refused, so we ran along the street, keeping to the shadows behind carts and barrels and the terrified horses hitched to the *ramadas* outside the store.

The Mexicans seemed to be after loot more than anything else and a few spirited Americans had now armed themselves with the nearest weapon to hand. I saw a man pounding the head of a Mexican with a baseball bat until the Mexican's cries for mercy died. Across the street, three more of them were trying to break into a doorway. As we watched, it opened suddenly and a woman appeared with a huge pan. As the Mexicans tried to push past her, she flung the steaming contents full in their faces and they staggered back, screaming, clawing what looked like scalding soup from their eyes.

'I once stopped Injuns with a pan of boilin' water,' she shrieked. 'I can stop you!'

As the door slammed, one of the Mexicans snatched up his rifle and started firing, and Tommy dropped him in his tracks with a shot from his Mondragón, so that the other two Mexicans ran off into the darkness.

The main targets appeared to be the bank, the store and the livery stable. Mexicans were milling about outside in a confusion of men and horses, ducking as shots were fired at them from windows, and firing back whenever an opportunity offered. Then a pile of drums of petrol standing in the street outside the store suddenly exploded in flames as stray bullets struck them; blazing petrol flew in all directions, and I saw Mexicans stumbling away screaming, their clothes on fire.

The inhabitants of Camarillo seemed to be recovering their wits by this time. As the store went up and the street became as light as day, the old frontier experiences they'd imbibed with their mother's milk from survivors of the Indian wars took over, and the raiders clearly began to get the worst of it.

We had managed to push our way into a saddlery just down the street, and we could see the Mexicans against the flames clearly enough to identify them from the stray Americans running for cover. Every time they tried to rush the bank, they ran into a fusillade of shots not only from a room above the bank but from us as well. The town seemed to be riddled with bullets by this time because the one thing the Mexicans weren't short of was ammunition.

More than a few of them were stretched out in the dust now, however. Peering through a broken window, it occurred to me that I'd read all this in the Wild West books of Zane Grey which we'd all devoured with enthusiasm as boys. We were fighting bandits – even if they were Mexican bandits. It was a startling thought, especially coming as it did in the middle of all the shouting and shooting.

The Mexicans had decided to give up their attempt on the bank now and had moved to the other side of the square. I heard shouts and screams, then a whole bunch of them came crashing down the steps of what I took to be the hotel, because it was the only place that was ablaze with light. They jumped on their horses and, sped on their way by a last few shots, thundered out of the town. The fight appeared to be over.

Straightening up as the dust settled, we stared across the plaza. I could see at least eight bodies stretched out, lying in the grotesquerie of sudden death like broken dolls, their high-crowned sombreros giving them a final touch of macabre inconsequentiality. The townspeople collecting up the weapons looked grimy and dazed, trailing their rifles with the butts in the dust. A few were struggling to save the store but it was clearly hopeless and a few more were shouting as they fought to quench the flames at the back of the hotel.

Already the undertaker, dressed in a dark suit and wearing a black bowler, had driven out in a flat buggy on spidery wheels with his name – 'Jacob Dibben' – in large white letters on the side, and a man who appeared to be a doctor was bending over a body. As he shook his head, two men heaved the Mexican into the buggy and the undertaker moved on to the next one. Those who appeared to still be alive were dragged to their feet and hauled off to the jail by the Sheriff who appeared at last, festooned with revolvers, with a couple of his deputies.

It seemed to be about time to find Charley. Knowing her, I suspected she'd probably have enjoyed the fun, even if she'd spent most of the time under one of the beds or the billiard table. The hotel entrance was jammed with people and there were two dead Mexicans stretched in the dust at the bottom of the wide wooden steps. A bus stood at the side, its bodywork riddled with bullets, half its windows knocked out. Its proprietor, the man, I assumed, who'd brought the rail passengers to the border, was staring at it in bewilderment.

'You the chap who brought those people in from Mexico?' I asked him.

'Yeah. And I sure picked a fine time to arrive.'

'Where are they?'

'In the hotel. That's where I left 'em.'

'Were there two girls?'

'Sure was. And an old body whose husband got shot by Villa down Sonora way. They're all in there.'

They were just lifting the two dead Mexicans into the undertaker's waggon as we went inside. In the hall, a group of men was standing round another body which was lying behind an overturned table. I could see a pair of high-heeled boots and the ends of a snappy pair of Mexican trousers protruding.

'That guy Guzmán,' the landlord of the hotel was saying bitterly.

'Is that him?' Tommy asked.

'Nah. Not this one. This one's Encarnación Itarparcia, his side-kick. I've seen him before.' The landlord lifted a Winchester. 'Got him as they were running out of the door.' He jerked a hand and grinned proudly. 'Right from the top of the stairs there. Heard 'em running down and grabbed my pants and gun.'

'What were they after?' Tommy asked.

'Money, I guess. That's why they were trying to get in the bank.'

'Well,' Slingsby said, 'they didn't make much profit. They didn't get in the bank and they left four of 'em stretched on the sidewalk outside.'

Everybody seemed to be in a euphoric mood at having driven off the Mexicans. I brought them down to earth.

'What about the passengers from the train?' I demanded. 'Where are they?'

The landlord gestured. 'Around, I guess,' he said.

'We're looking for two of 'em. Two girls.'

'I saw 'em.' He gestured, still occupied with recounting his defence of his property. 'They shared a room. We had one left and the guys said they could have it. Them and the old lady. The guys said they'd sleep on the billiard table. When them Mexes came—'

'Where are they?' I interrupted. Suddenly, an odd prickly sensation of worry had started. Now that the shooting had stopped I was surprised that there was no sign of Charley.

'Well, they probably slept through it!'

'Not on your damn life,' I said. 'Not Charley! What room were they in?'

'Number Seven. But don't you go busting in there, bud! This is a respectable house!'

'Well, go up yourself,' I snapped. 'Or send your wife or something.'

'Who the hell are you, son?' The landlord was becoming aggressive, but I was afraid suddenly and in no mood to worry what he thought.

'Never mind who he is,' Tommy said. 'Do as he says.' The landlord was obviously quite prepared to accept orders from Tommy, whose accent identified him as a compatriot, and he went into the kitchen. A woman appeared, her hair tousled, her clothes looking as though she'd flung them on in a hurry.

'I'm not going up there alone,' she said. 'One of them *dagos* is probably waiting on the landing.'

In the end the landlord went up with her, holding his rifle at the ready, and stood at the top of the stairs as she disappeared along the corridor.

Everybody had become silent now and the group round the body of the Mexican had stopped chattering. The undertaker had arrived but he was waiting silently until things started to move again. I caught Tommy looking at me, his face suddenly worried, and Puddy, tall, slender, blond, his eyes concerned. Slingsby's cherubic face had changed, as it always did at times like this, and there were unexpected hard planes and bleak angles you didn't often see.

After a while the landlord's wife reappeared. She was leading a middle-aged woman in black, who was weeping. There was no sign of Charley and my heart went cold inside me.

'They came up the stairs,' the woman in black was sobbing. 'They took every bit of money I possessed. Everything my husband left me and all my jewels. Then I heard them arguing with the girls next door. When they'd gone I went in. There was nobody there. Those two poor girls! I don't know who they were but I brought the labels off their luggage. Somebody ought to do something about it.'

The landlord had taken the labels from her. 'Dominique Duellin—' he pronounced it 'Dominic Dewlin' '—French, I guess. And—' he paused and peered more closely at the other label. 'Gee-gosh!' he said.

He looked round at the crowd who were staring at him. 'Charlotte Margaret Caroline Bartelott-Dyveton-Sykes.' He gave a nervous grin. 'That sure is some handle. Who in tarnation is she?'

'I'll tell you who she is,' I said grimly. 'She's my girl, Charley. And I think we'd better start doing something about finding her.'

Chapter 3

Out in the middle of the vast ridged plain, half a day's ride from anywhere, lay a little salty marsh. It covered several acres and growing from it were a few withered-looking plants which Tommy said the Mexicans called *tules.* The country looked like a huge dead beast, tawny-coloured and lean, and the seven of us, as we made our way among the ridges, seemed to be picking our way among its ribs.

We were hardly a posse, because there was only the Sheriff, one of his deputies, a vengeful man whose wife had been cut by flying glass, and the four of us from Europe – one American, two Englishmen and a Russian. We had no real idea what we intended, but we'd borrowed horses and splashed across a ford in the Rio Grande in the hope of catching up with Guzmán's *bandidos* before they'd gone so far we'd lose them altogether.

We'd picked up a bloodstained rag and then a sombrero, and eventually we found the carcass of a horse lying among the brushwood. Not long afterwards, we found a hastily scraped grave and inside it, as the Sheriff kicked the stones away, the body of a Mexican. He looked no more than fifteen, but Mexican troops, it seemed, were no respecters of age and they usually contained men from the age of puberty to grandfatherhood. Thousands of them had been swept from their farms by the revolution and, after ten years of it, this boy might well have wandered into Chihuahua where we were now right from the south round Morelos, Guerrero or Oaxaca.

The pace we'd made hadn't been set by the Sheriff or even by Tommy, but by me, with Tommy panting alongside to give directions. We hadn't spared the horses and they were as jaded now as we were. But it hadn't taken me long to realize that the all-out speed I'd first set was useless and, afterwards, knowing less about horses than about aeroplanes, I'd been more cautious and willing to accept Tommy's advice.

The immensity of the land was frightening. It was a series of enormous plateaux called *mesas*, each from four to ten miles wide, separated by narrow valleys running north and south, with long narrow fissures called *arroyos* leading from the level of the plateaux down into their depths. Beyond, the mountains lifted, golden bronze in the pitiless sunshine.

Dropping down into yet another valley as the dusty road wound and twisted in the stifling heat, I turned to the Sheriff.

'How far does this road go?' I said.

'Hell, all the way to Gutíerrez de Santa María.'

'Know it?'

'No, son. And I don't want to. I've been across the border some but I don't want to explore Mexico. Since the fight at Columbus the government don't encourage it and I reckon we ought to get back. I'm not enjoying this.'

'Those girls won't be enjoying it either,' I snapped.

He frowned, worried. 'I got no authority to be here,' he said.

'Then go back, dammit!' Tommy snapped. 'We'll do it on our own.'

The Sheriff looked uncomfortable. My hatred for him sprang not from any inefficiency on his part but from my worry for Charley, and I could see he wasn't a young man any more. Quite apart from his concern about doing something that might lose him his job, he was grey-faced with exhaustion. I glanced at the other two men. They weren't young either but had joined us probably as much as anything because they didn't want us to get ourselves killed.

I tried to speak as calmly as I could. 'Leave us your water bottles and food,' I said, 'and any spare ammunition. You'd better go back. Your government can't do anything to *us* – at least not to three of us – because we aren't Americans.'

The Sheriff seemed glad of the excuse but he was still reluctant to leave. In the end Tommy said he'd accept responsibility. We were guests in his house and what we did was his affair. In the end the Sheriff was placated, and they handed over all they could spare. Then Tommy wrote down his address on an envelope he dragged from an inside pocket. 'Get in touch with my father at San José,' he said. 'He'll be down with help. Money. Horses. People. Tell him what's happened. He'll know what to do.'

'Okay.'

'What's ahead?' I asked.

'Hell, son—' the Sheriff shrugged '—nothing. Just land. First town you come to's Acizpe del Oro but it ain't as big as Camarillo even.'

They turned their horses with a show of reluctance, but I guessed none of them was unhappy about returning to their own side of the border. I'd been long enough in Texas already to know that nobody trusted the Mexicans. In the last few years, there had been too many pointless murders of the American and British engineers who'd been brought in to run the Mexican railways and other industries. No American fancied going too deeply into this harsh haggard land without protection.

'It's best this way,' the Sheriff said as he paused for a last word before leaving. 'This ain't Columbus and we don't want another ruckus like that. The government wants to avoid trouble. There ain't a cat in hell's chance of catching 'em and they'll more'n likely try to ambush you, so look out. It's a case for the army and I'll send a guy over to El Paso to let 'em know.'

As they jogged off north again, we turned towards the south and, without even bothering to discuss the matter, kicked our horses into a trot.

Shortly afterwards we came to Acizpe del Oro. As the Sheriff had suggested, to call it a town was an exaggeration. It consisted of a single dusty street lined with *adobe* houses and wooden huts, a *cantina*, a shabby hotel, an enormous church and a large central building where the Mexican flag hung with a large framed portrait of a fat man with glasses, moustache and beard, who turned out to be President Carranza. It was the Mexican equivalent of the town hall and, as we stopped, the mayor and his council appeared to meet us. The mayor was a small fat man with spectacles, a large smile and a larger moustache, wearing a tricolour sash. He hadn't seen Guzmán or his band but he offered us a lecture on the future of Mexico in a mixture of English and Spanish.

'First Chief Carranza will triumph,' he insisted. 'I am Jesús Gregorio Gamboa and I am a Carrancista. We have been robbed by Rurales, Federales, Villistas, Maderistas, Huertistas, Obregónistas and every other kind of villain. The First Chief will put things right.'

'I hope Villa never comes this way,' Tommy observed dryly as we continued. 'He doesn't like Carrancistas.'

We kept on moving. Ravines, sharp-edged as knife-wounds, cut across the *mesquite*-matted slopes, and skirting them was hard work, with either side of the road covered with cactus and Spanish bayonet. By evening we'd seen neither hide nor hair of the Mexican *bandidos* and we had to stop because it was growing dark. Tommy chose a small basin-like valley with a flat face of rock we could get our backs against if we had to and we pulled off the saddles and fed the horses, picking out the pebbles that always appeared in Mexican grain. When we'd rubbed them down with wads of dry grass, we didn't bother to cook because we were too tired, and instead chewed on cold meat and lumps of frying-pan bread we'd been given in Camarillo before we'd set off.

Sitting with my back to a rock, I studied the mountains ahead, my mind numb. Charley and I had spent little enough time in each other's company in the last year or two. I'd known her around three years now and most of that time I'd been far from her side – flying in France and then in Russia. But it had been Charley who'd nursed me back to health and sanity when the Germans had almost blown my head off just before the Armistice, and she had the most tremendous faith in me. I'd never thought of myself as much of a catch for any girl but she'd always insisted I was going to end up a general, and I could only assume that she either knew what she was talking about or had an incredible amount of belief in me. Neither of us was very demonstrative and since I'd suggested in a wave of affection for her in 1918 that we get married, I'd often wondered if I were right. We'd both still been too young – and probably still were – to be classed as responsible adults, although Charley had done nursing through two major assaults, and I'd flown in France since 1915 and come out with a string of gongs that was enough to weigh me down. But we'd clung together nevertheless, never losing touch despite the odds, still warm towards each other, and it was the fact, I think, that if anything went wrong now she might not be around when I wanted her that worried me most and convinced me that any doubts I'd ever had about us were wrong. Charley and I, despite our casualness, despite our post-war sophistication – which, I suspected, we largely put on to prove to other people that we were older than we were – needed each other; just to be around, to reply to letters, to provide a shoulder to weep on.

I came awake with a start to realize that I'd dozed off. It wasn't daylight but there was something about the horizon to indicate that the day wasn't far away. I glanced at my watch and sat up to see Tommy watching me.

'I'd be happier if this were the army, Brat,' he said.

'So would I,' I admitted. 'I'd be happier still if it weren't Charley we were chasing. Makes it a bit more personal when it's somebody you know and you're fond of.'

'Yeah.' He nodded agreement. 'That's right. But I have a feeling that Guzmán's boys aren't far away.'

'Why?'

'Hell of a lot of owls hooting around here last night.'

'You mean they weren't owls?'

'Noises don't make themselves. Besides, this isn't owl country. No trees. Owls don't live in rock faces.'

What he said made sense. 'You think this blasted Splendid Ben, or whatever he calls himself, is watching us?'

'Shouldn't be surprised.'

It was unnerving but Puddy took the same view. He'd already lived through one revolution and a civil war, and had been conscious every time he stood in front of his men that some mutinous Russian peasant might drive a bullet into his back, so his senses were heightened by experience. He looked so tense it seemed that if you'd plucked him he'd have twanged.

'I agree with Tommy,' he said. 'I think there are people all round us, watching us.'

'Where?'

He gestured at the slope and fissures of the canyon we were in. 'It wouldn't take very much doing, good Bratty, to hide a regiment up there. They can see the dust we make from twenty miles away during the day and at night they can close in on us if they wish.'

'You want to go back? Like the Sheriff and his pals?'

Puddy stared at me, his face grave. 'Yes,' he said bluntly. 'I think there is nothing else we can do, sitting on our horses, with nothing but four rifles to back us up.'

'You forgotten Charley?'

'No, my good Bratty,' he said gravely, 'I haven't. But I have the suspicion that we have gone into this thing without thinking much about it. I think it will need more than four men, four horses, four rifles and a lot of faith.'

Even I had to admit that he was talking sense.

'We'll give it a go today,' I said. 'If we turn nothing up, we'll go back.'

'I think Puddy's right, Brat,' Slingsby said. 'We must be twenty-odd miles inside Mexico now.'

When it grew light enough to move, we ate a cold breakfast and saddled up. We were stiff with riding now and the horses weren't in much better shape. But, my mind numb with worry, I couldn't bring myself to stop. Round the next corner, I kept telling myself; they'd be round the next corner, abandoned by the Mexicans because they were scared of us catching them up. Dirty, perhaps; tired; hungry without doubt; but just left behind for us to find.

But they weren't of course. Every corner was like the last one. A dry dusty view with *mesquite*, cactus and a few sparse trees. And nothing else.

I was growing more and more aware of Puddy's worry. His eyes were all over the place. Just after daylight the wind came up and swept along the *mesas*, moving the dust, changing the shapes of the hummocks under the dark *mesquite*. It blew across the bare slopes, over the summits of the mountains, and down to a desert river flowing south through a canyon where the hills were steep to the edge of the water, moving the dagger-points of the stiff-rooted soapweed and clacking the seeds in the pods on the brittle stalks.

We pushed on all that morning, the wind growing stronger as the sun lifted higher. The sky turned amber and we had to tie handkerchieves over our mouths against the coppery dust. The light crashed against granite, mica, limestone, and basalt, and we had to squint in the glare. *Arroyos* deep as wounds were all round us, their depths driven by the harsh sun into sand and pebbles, where only *chamiso*, thorny *agrito*, *mesquite* cactus and Spanish bayonet would grow. There seemed to be only two colours – brown and grey.

There was no talk now, just the squeak of leather, the chink of bits and the huff-puff of the horses' breathing, and we rode stiff and swaying in the saddle. We'd just about had enough. '*Sin tierra y sin ley*' – landless and lawless – that was how I'd heard Mexico described more than once and I felt I could add '*sin benevolencia*' – without kindness. It was one of the harshest countries I'd ever seen.

'We aren't getting anywhere,' Tommy said. His voice came unexpectedly, flat and arid and despairing, and I knew he was right.

Puddy was looking round him, his eyes moving across the landscape as if he suspected that somewhere beyond the dust there were enemies. Slingsby's boyish face was narrow and wedge-shaped with tiredness and anger. Then unexpectedly, just when we were beginning to think of turning back, the wind dropped and we bumped into a Mexican sitting on a heavy cart pulled by an ox. We fell on him as if he were a gift from heaven.

'Mexicans?' I said. '*Bandidos?*'

He gaped at me until Tommy took over. '*Donde son los bandidos?*' he asked in Spanish that left a lot to be desired but was obviously intelligible to the Mexican crouching against the glare, his sombrero pulled over his eyes, his *sarape* wound round his throat against the dust the wheels stirred up.

'*Bandidos, señor?*'

'*Esplenderoso Guzmán.*'

'*Donde?* Where is he?'

The old Mexican was clearly disinclined to help. Though one of Tommy's twenty-dollar bills would normally have worked wonders, this time he would say no more than that he'd seen the Mexicans pass, thirty or so of them, *más o menos* – more or less – with two *gringas señoritas*, all on horseback and heading south.

'Where will they be now?'

The Mexican shrugged.

'Come on,' I said. 'Let's push on.'

'We haven't a chance, Brat,' Slingsby said.

'We can try,' I growled.

'Not on these nags, Brat,' Tommy pointed out. 'And the further we go the further we are from help.'

I knew they were right but I didn't wish to back off. 'We can go a *bit* further.'

Tommy interrupted. 'Brat,' he said. 'I know how you feel. By gosh, I do. But this is silly. We can't do a damn thing. What can four tired men on four jaded horses do to thirty-odd *bandidos* who've probably slept well and eaten well? We could only put the girls' lives in danger. The only thing we can sensibly do, I guess, is back off and see what my Old Man has to say. He knows what goes on around here. He's fought off marauding Mexicans and Indians half his life. He'll know how to handle it.' His face twisted in his concern. 'It's the only thing, Brat. What we're doing can only cause harm.'

'And—' Puddy put in his twopennyworth '—there is always the chance we might not be lucky enough to get back to the border *alive*.'

We all whipped round. 'What do you mean?' Slingsby said.

'We have been watched for the last hour.'

'How do you know?'

Puddy shrugged. It was something he couldn't explain. 'I've seen dust. Perhaps it's the smell.'

'You can *smell* 'em?' Slingsby asked.

'I can sense them. I always knew in Russia when there were Bolsheviks about. I don't know why, but I was rarely wrong. I think we had better turn back.'

Since I could hardly go on alone, I had to agree. It took some doing, though. The thought of Charley in the hands of a gang of *bandidos* was hard to swallow. But even I could see that arriving at Splendid Ben's camp alone – or even with three companions – wasn't going to achieve much. We'd probably only add to his captives – if he didn't murder us first.

We hadn't gone more than a mile in reverse when the first shot was fired. It came from nowhere and stirred up a puff of dust just ahead of us.

Nobody said anything. We just put spurs to the jaded horses and pushed them from a canter to a gallop. After a while, when we felt safe, we slowed down again. We had a long way to go and you can't gallop a horse for ever. I'd heard of men driving a horse until it died, but it wouldn't have showed much sense because it would have been a great deal harder for us trying to ride two-up.

We'd just decided we'd thrown off whoever it was who'd been watching us when there was another shot. It was well wide this time but once more we set off at a gallop. The horses were failing now. They'd been at it almost continuously and they needed rest.

'Good job the Mexicans are such rotten shots,' Tommy said, trying to cheer us up.

Once again we slowed down and for the rest of the day we had no further trouble. We found a stream where we let the horses drink and nibble at the sparse brown grass, while we ate what was left of our food and squatted down for the night among the rocks. It was Tommy who suggested we ought to post a sentry.

'You never know, the blighters might try to pinch the nags,' he said.

He agreed to take first watch and I relieved him. As I was sitting in the dark hugging the Mondragón I'd picked up in Camarillo I realized how tired we must all be. Despite all my efforts, my eyes insisted on closing, and I started to wakefulness again and again as I felt my eyelids drooping.

I was glad when my two hours finished and I'd just moved towards Slingsby, who was to take over from me, when I heard the clatter of a stone. Putting my hand hard over his mouth, I shook him gently. His eyes opened and he looked up at me, his eyes questioning.

'Quiet,' I whispered. 'We've got visitors. Wake the others.'

As he slithered off to where Tommy and Puddy were sleeping, I moved silently among the rocks to the horses. As I drew near them I heard the shuffle and clink of hooves against the stone, then I heard a distinct click, and it was one I'd heard so many times I knew exactly what it was. It was somebody cocking a gun.

Crouching among the rocks, I tried to see in the dark. My eyes had grown accustomed to it by this time and eventually I saw a movement, then the towering conical shape of a sombrero. The Mexicans had come to steal the horses.

We'd already suffered enough humiliation but shooting a man in cold blood came hard. I'd shot one in Camarillo, but there'd been a fight going on at the time and I'd suspected then it was a case of him or me. Now it was different, so I reversed the Mondragón and grasped it by the muzzle. As the Mexican drew nearer I stepped out.

'*Cuerpo de Cristo!*'

He seemed surprised to find anybody awake but, before he could bolt, the rifle clumped satisfyingly against his head and he went over backwards like a shot rabbit. Only then did I realize there were several others in the darkness among the rocks and I reversed the rifle and pulled the trigger. The shot echoed and re-echoed round the *arroyo* and suddenly the night went mad. There seemed to be bullets flying everywhere, striking the rocks and whining off into the distance.

As I dodged for shelter, I slipped. Before I knew where I was a Mexican was standing over me and I was staring into the muzzle of a revolver that looked like a six-inch cannon. I'd just decided I was never going to have the pleasure of seeing Charley again – or anything else either – when a rifle exploded by my ear. I felt the heat of the flame and the Mexican staggered back, caught his foot against a stone, and flopped down, spreadeagled and staring at the sky.

There was another flurry of shots and the clatter of hooves, then Slingsby yanked me to my feet.

'I thought I was a goner then,' I said.

'So did I. I'm afraid our friend *is*.'

The Mexican was quite dead and as the light increased we scraped a hole, pushed him into it and piled rocks on top against the coyotes. We found his horse stumbling among the rocks, its foot through the reins, and as the man I'd hit with the rifle was still moaning against a rock, we bound up his jaw, which Tommy decided was broken, with his own neckerchief. After relieving him of rifle and pistol, we pushed him into the saddle and sent him off south. Feeling the way I did, hating every Mexican who drew breath, I'd happily have left him where he was.

We mounted again, having first smashed the rifles we'd taken against the rocks, and set off again north towards the border. I would never have believed how tired I could become. The path was dusty and the horses were stumbling with weariness.

Acizpe del Oro turned out to watch us pass, mostly soft-eyed girls, bare-footed children and old men, with Mayor Gamboa and his friends on the steps of his office calling slogans at us.

'*Viva Mexico*,' he yelled. '*Maten los traidores!* Long live Mexico! Kill the traitors! The chickpea vendor, Obregón, will never survive when First Chief Carranza returns!'

We were in no mood to discuss the niceties of Mexican politics and we cantered past without even looking at him.

'Another hour or two and we'll be safe,' Tommy said.

I couldn't bring myself to answer. More than our safety was at stake, it seemed to me.

The horses had slowed to a stumbling walk now, and we could actually see the glint of water when the Mexicans came again, appearing out of the scrub bush like a charge of cavalry. One of them wore a bowler hat and a city suit but he was festooned with ammunition belts. Another, in the white dirty cotton of a *peón*, looked old enough to be my grandfather, but he was yelling and shrieking like the rest and firing his rifle with the same abandon. The others wore a mixture of clothing, one in wide Mexican trousers with buttons down the side, another in a long overcoat that came to his ankles, another in hip-high leather leggings. Four of them wore sombreros, I noticed, and two or three pointed khaki hats such as

New Zealand soldiers wore; I guessed they'd picked them up from some quartermaster's store Pershing's cavalrymen had left behind in 1916, or bought them cheap from some American salesman standing on his right to make a living. But whatever they wore, they all seemed to be festooned with weapons and it was only their rotten shooting that stopped any of us being hit.

We clapped heels to the worn-out horses and clattered towards the distant stretch of water, the Mexicans howling after us. Tommy was using a revolver he'd taken from the dead Mexican and I saw one of our pursuers go head-over-heels over the tail of his pony; then, his foot caught in the stirrups, bounce away over the stony soil, his head in the dust as the animal made off madly away from the din. Another one came at me swinging a sabre he'd got from God alone knew where. Holding my rifle like a revolver, I shoved it in his chest and pulled the trigger. I didn't see what happened to him because something hit me on the shoulder and almost spun me out of the saddle, but then we were through the line of Mexicans and I saw at least three horses with empty saddles blundering away across the plain.

As we hurtled towards the river, Slingsby's horse went down with a crash in front of me. I heaved on the reins and he grabbed the stirrup.

'Get up behind,' I yelled.

'No,' he screamed. 'Keep going!'

And clinging to the stirrup, like the Highlanders at Waterloo, he ran alongside me in giant strides as the horse drew him along with it. We might never have got away, even so, but Puddy – Baron Alexei Ivanovitch Yazheskov-Pudhovkhin himself – swung his horse round suddenly and tore headlong into the following Mexicans. They were so startled they scattered, and I saw two of the smaller Mexican ponies go down before the heavy shoulders of his mount. As one of them rose to his feet, pointing a revolver, Puddy brought his rifle down on his head and he collapsed among the rocks, while Puddy wheeled his horse and crashed through them yet again after us. By the time he caught us up, Slingsby had scrambled up behind me.

'Thanks, Puddy,' I yelled.

He gave a thin smile. 'Before I am an aviator,' he said, 'I am in the Empress Alexandra's Lancers. We are a crack cavalry regiment.'

As we reached the river, I saw Americans on the other side, carrying rifles. They set up such a barrage of shots at the men following us that the Mexicans bolted for cover and we splashed across the shallows until we stopped on American soil. Even as I hauled on the reins, the horse went down on its knees, blowing up the dust in little jets that mingled with the foam from its mouth, and Slingsby and I went over its head.

When I came round, the horse was on its feet and was already beginning to look better as a woman gave it brandy.

'More'n a guy can git since prohibition,' the Sheriff said bitterly.

He seemed to want to discuss what had happened, but I pretended I hadn't heard him and we stumbled into Camarillo, aware of defeat. A few Mexicans had lost their lives and doubtless more than one horse had been ruined, but we'd achieved precisely nothing.

–

The town had already begun its clean-up after the raid and had buried its dead – one man who'd shot himself by accident with his own gun and an old woman who'd died of heart failure. There were two or three wounded, mostly hit by flying glass, but on the whole the place had got off lightly; they could claim ten dead Mexicans apart from the ones we'd disposed of beyond the border. Judging by the extravagant claims, several thousand more were likely to drop dead on their way home from their wounds. The undertaker had already commandeered an extra buggy and was taking the bodies that had been left behind out into the desert to bury them.

The town looked cold and grey in the early morning, the charred store and the back of the hotel blackened by the flames. The owner of the bus was still bewailing his loss but one or two people had acquired new rifles and at least fourteen Mexican ponies had been left behind and had already been claimed by men who were insisting loudly that their own had been stolen.

The Stutz was just where we'd left it in front of the hotel. We were standing alongside it, bleak-faced and exhausted, when the big Franklin appeared, with Tommy's father, Evalina, and two of his ranch hands. The big vehicle slid to a stop in the dust and the old man climbed stiffly out.

'You all okay?' he asked.

'Thanks to Puddy,' Tommy said. 'It looked a bit dicey back there, but he went in for a bit of cavalry tactics that stopped 'em dead.'

Evalina gave Puddy an adoring look, and we were still trying to make our tired brains work out our next move when an old man appeared riding on a mule. He was Mexican and he wore the usual white cotton clothes and a huge straw sombrero.

'Kill him,' somebody said in a fury of hatred for the people across the border who had inflicted the disaster on them.

'Hold your jaw, Sam Ferrabee,' the Sheriff said. 'I know this guy. It's El Cojo – the Cripple, Indalecio Blazio. He's deaf, dumb, half blind and has a twisted leg. He wouldn't hurt a fly, even if he could.'

The mule, which was as old as the man on its back, shuffled to a stop and the Mexican slid to the ground. Taking off his sombrero and holding it to his chest in the humble but dignified manner so many of the Mexican *peóns* had, he bowed before the Sheriff and handed him a sheet of paper.

With infuriating deliberation, the Sheriff, who was slow-moving and fat, fished out a pair of steel-framed spectacles and perched them on his nose.

'It's from Guzmán,' he said, peering at the paper. 'He's got them two girls all right. He says they'll come to no harm, providing the proper ransom's paid.'

'How much?' Tommy's father said at once. 'If it's good American cash-money he wants, we've got it.'

'No,' the Sheriff said, looking a little startled. ''T'ain't cash-money. It's rifles. He says he aims to destroy Obregón and he wants four hundred Springfield rifles with the ammunition to go with them.'

Dan Tucker's jaw dropped. 'He can't have *that*!' he said. 'He'd be back here next night to set the place afire!'

'That's what he says.'

Old Tucker scowled. 'Even if we had 'em,' he growled, 'the government would never permit it.'

The army arrived soon afterwards, a company of cavalrymen armed to the teeth and mounted on Morgans. Their uniforms and equipment were the old pre-war issue, olive-drab flannel shirts, breeches, sweaters and canvas leggings, and peaked campaign hats with wide brims and chinstraps, which made them look like boy scouts. They carried .45 pistols low on their right thighs, and round their necks they wore large neckerchieves they could raise over their noses and mouths against the dust. Most of them also had motoring goggles of amber celluloid round their hats against the dust and the glare.

The Captain in command was an oak-faced man of forty-odd. His name was O'Hara and his Irish accent was thick enough to cut with a knife. I suspected, in fact, that he laid it on deliberately, because he looked as though he'd worked his way up from the ranks. Probably because of this, he was more than ever conscious of what his orders were. He'd taken a long time to reach his present rank and he had no intention of taking any chances. He was there to protect Camarillo, not go charging off into Mexico after a couple of kidnapped girls.

'You're supposed to be the greatest nation on earth,' I snarled at him furiously. 'You're always telling the rest of the world so, anyway! Why don't you behave as if you were?'

It was unfair, I realized immediately. He had his orders and it was more than his career was worth to go against them. Since Villa's last defeat in 1919 at Juárez, the frontier had been quiet and the United States didn't want to stir it up again. It certainly wanted no more punitive expeditions crashing across the border, not even at company strength, and the Captain was immovable.

Slingsby snorted. 'What a way for Yanks to behave,' he said.

'Who's Yanks?' The speaker was an old man with a white beard who wore a long grey coat and a faded old-fashioned *képi* with a yellow band round it.

O'Hara turned to him. 'Who're you?' he snapped.

'Lukey Morro.' The old man pointed to a youngster sitting on a motor bicycle. 'That's my grandson, and I was riding with Jeb Stuart's cavalry when he was shot at Yellow Tavern in 'sixty-four, before you were born.' He peered angrily at O'Hara then turned to Slingsby. 'He might be a Yank, son,' he went on, 'but Camarillo's south of the Mason-Dixon line and we're Southerners – rebels – and we spent four years fighting Yanks. We still are, I guess, because we ain't had a damn thing from them guys in Washington since Lee surrendered at Appomatox. I was sixteen before I realized "Damn Yankee" was two words.'

Something had to be said to lessen the tension. O'Hara was frowning and so was Tommy's father. Evalina, who was a pretty girl and managed to look fetching despite the hour in a wide black *chihuahueno* hat and a divided leather riding skirt, was giving Slingsby a hurt look.

'I'm sorry,' I said to O'Hara. 'We shouldn't have gone off at half-cock like that. It wasn't fair. I'm an officer myself and I know what orders are.'

Captain O'Hara accepted the apology placidly and tried to put things right. 'That's okay, son,' he said. 'But my orders are explicit. I stay this side of the border and take care of Camarillo and the women and kids.'

'There's one possibility,' Dan Tucker pointed out. 'I have a contact over the border. Guy called Ojarra, Emiliano Ojarra.' He smiled and indicated the Captain. 'Same family as yours, I guess, Captain. Bog Irish.'

The Captain looked indignant and old Tucker explained. 'There are one or two Mexes with Irish names. Obregón's one. He claims descent from

Miguel Obregón, once known as Michael O'Brien, Irish bodyguard to the last of the Spanish viceroys in Mexico. Ojarra's another. O'Brien had a *compañero* called Patrick O'Hara, later known as Patricio Ojarra. This one joined Madero in 1910 against Díaz but he grew sick of Villa's excesses and retired. Because he was wounded in the fighting he's respected, and they leave him alone. I've bought cattle from him. He'll help.'

'How?'

Old Tucker looked baffled for a minute. 'I guess we'd better leave that to him,' he admitted. 'I'll send one of my Mexes to find him.'

Tommy scowled. 'What do we do until then?' he demanded.

Captain O'Hara frowned. 'Sir, these two girls aren't even Americans. One's French, I'm told, and one's English.'

'Surely,' Tommy said, 'You're not proposing to let that put you off?'

The Captain looked worried. 'Son,' he said. 'It looks to me like an affair for the British Consul. There's one in El Paso and they told me he'd be coming down here – quick sharp.'

'They were kidnapped from American soil,' I snorted.

The Captain looked apologetic. 'Listen, son—'

'Don't call me "son",' I snapped at him. It was something that happened often, because I still wasn't very old, and it always infuriated me.

The Captain stiffened. 'I'm sorry – sir! I'll level with you. We're Custer's lot and since we were wiped out at Little Big Horn we don't take kindly to being pushed around, and if I had my way, I'd be across that border chop-chop and doing what I could. But I was with Pershing at Guerrero, and I was there to pick up the dead after Boyd's charge at Carrizal. And if you want my opinion, which I guess you don't, then I reckon it'll need more than a single troop of the Seventh Cavalry to find this guy, Guzmán.'

Chapter 4

The Consul arrived from El Paso the following morning. He was a languid smooth-faced man in glasses, but he knew exactly what was what because he'd been looking after British interests ever since the revolutionary wars had started south of the border.

His name was Lea-Ferney and he wore a high stiff collar, a carnation in his buttonhole and what Slingsby insisted was an old Etonian tie. But there was nothing effete about him.

'You'll not get the American government involved,' he said at once. 'Pershing's expedition was an abysmal failure and all Americans with any sense know it was. The *New York Herald* said it was a farce from the American standpoint and an eyesore to the Mexicans, and they withdrew it after nine months. Its cost was enormous and its only visible signs of success were twenty-one prisoners and a small quantity of captured arms. Indeed, people were provoked into asking why it was called a *punitive* expedition since nobody got punished.' He drew a deep breath. 'In my humble opinion it was a record of barren futility and the United States government have no wish to see it repeated.'

It was a pretty little speech but it wasn't much help to me.

'There are two girls over the border there,' I pointed out as calmly as I could. 'One of them English, one of them French. The Americans tell us it's none of their affair, despite the fact that they were kidnapped from American soil which, I'd have thought, ought to be enough to rouse some sentiment of indignation in them. Since it doesn't appear to, what about the British and French governments? What are they proposing to do?'

'What do you suggest, Major Falconer?'

I didn't really know what to suggest and fell back on the old snobbish values of family and influence.

'You know who the English girl is?' I asked.

Lea-Ferney nodded gravely. 'While I can't claim to know the young lady as well as you, who appear to be engaged to her, I *can* claim to have met her. I was at school with her father, you see, and, since you're in the Royal Air Force, you've probably met my godson, Ludovic Sykes.'

I stared at him, startled. The damn man not only knew Charley but he was godfather to my old friend and CO, Ludo Sykes.

Slingsby was looking angry. 'They used to send a gunboat when anythin' like this used to happen,' he snorted.

'That was in the last century,' Lea-Ferney said dryly. 'And how do you suggest they send a gunboat into inland Mexico?'

Slingsby glared. 'Won't the damn government do anythin'?' he asked.

'They'll send a strong protest to Mexico City.'

'Is that all?'

Lea-Ferney shrugged. 'There've been plenty of British residents kidnapped – even murdered – in Mexico in the last ten years,' he pointed out. 'And plenty of French, too. Neither nation did anything about them, partly because we were rather involved in a major war with the Germans, as you'll doubtless, from your military titles, be aware. But it's not simply that. There's no official government in Mexico. There hasn't been a genuine government since Díaz fell in 1910, because nobody hung on long enough; and in any case their authority never stretched much further than Mexico City or the land where their troops were encamped.'

'Do you mean we can't even protest?'

'Who to?' Lea-Ferney asked. 'Carranza's been thrown out of office and, at this moment, as far as I can tell, he's a fugitive somewhere between Mexico

City and Veracruz. In the meantime, Obregón, who seems to be the next likelihood for the office of president, hasn't yet reached the capital.'

What he said made sense. You could hardly protest to the Mexican government when there wasn't a Mexican government.

Lea-Ferney drew a deep breath. 'I shall do what I can, of course,' he said. 'Because obviously no responsible American will let guns go to Guzmán after what happened in Columbus and Juárez and here. I expect the British government to register a protest, but they're still a little preoccupied with the peace in Europe, the possibility of a new war in the Levant, and the troubles in Ireland, so I doubt if they'll be prepared to follow it up. You might say roughly the same conditions apply to the French and the Americans.'

'Can't you offer anything better than that?'

Lea-Ferney shrugged. 'Since Mexico has no real government, it also has no real law,' he observed. 'Its army commanders are the real rulers but, as they're still involved with trying to kill each other, they haven't much time to be concerned with intrusions from north of the border.'

'What are you getting at?' Tommy growled.

'Why not fit out an expedition yourself? While I can do little officially, I might do something privately.

I'm a wealthy man and I could put funds at your disposal.'

'They don't need funds,' Tommy's father snapped. 'We've got plenty.'

I stared at him and then at Lea-Ferney. He seemed to be giving us the green light to set up a rescue operation and I decided we ought to take him up. 'In that case,' I said quickly, 'what are we waiting for? Let's get cracking.'

–

After our hurried gallop into Mexico we were more wary this time. We decided that perhaps the best thing we could do was use the Franklin. It could do around sixty miles an hour on a good road and we felt its huge wheels could handle the rough Mexican terrain.

But we couldn't all get into the Franklin, and Dan Tucker suggested sending the Stutz back to San José for one or two more of his men. He had accepted that, even if the affair was no business of the British, French or American governments, it was certainly his, and he seemed to feel the need for a few more of his own people about him. Sniffing round Camarillo, he returned with a brand-new Ford, brass-bonneted and black. It was new enough to have a little notice on the dashboard – 'To obtain best results, this car should not be driven faster than twenty miles an hour for the first five-hundred miles.'

'That don't matter at all,' Tucker said. 'The guy I bought it off said it had already done a thousand.'

There was a carrier at the back for two spare tyres and a luggage rack on the right-hand running board, and the radiator was crowned with a motormeter, a glass-faced instrument which gave the temperature inside the bonnet and was marked with 'Good Average', 'Higher Efficiency' and 'Danger, Steaming'.

'Cost me four hundred dollars,' Tucker said. 'Since it only cost three-sixty new, the guy didn't argue. He just climbed out and I climbed in.'

We decided that the two cars should go together, me driving the Franklin and Tommy the Ford, which looked a much more tricky proposition. I was to have Slingsby and Puddy with me, while Tommy was to have the hands old Tucker had brought with him, two middle-aged men with small sinewy frames and legs so bowed they looked as if they'd been born on a horse. Their names were Archie MacTaggart, which showed a good Scottish descent, and Snake-Eyes Callison. They looked as alike as twins.

For safety, the old man promised to raise a small posse, made up if necessary of his own hands, to back us up and fetch us out if trouble occurred.

'And I'll be here,' Evalina said. 'Looking after things this side of the border.'

'Such as what?' Tommy said.

She pushed back the *chihuahueno* hat. 'I guess when those two poor girls arrive, they'll need to be looked after. They'll need a change of clothes and a bath, at least. You men never think of that.'

While we were loading the cars and checking their engines, under the supervision of the old Civil War veteran's motor-cycling grandson, Young Lukey, another message arrived from across the border, brought the same way as the last one – by the old deaf and dumb Mexican cripple on the limping mule. The beast looked ancient, the deep cavities above its eyes matching those of the old man himself.

It was another message from Guzmán, and it informed us that from the kindness of his heart he was permitting the young English lady to address a letter to her beloved.

It was in Mexican Spanish, of course, but it was well written and those were the exact words. With it was a letter addressed to 'Major Martin Falconer' and my heart leapt as I recognized Charley's handwriting.

'Dear Martin,' she wrote. 'I seem to have landed myself well and truly in the *soup*... I might have been wiser if I'd come to meet you by *sea*!!! However, this beastly little *Dago* who's holding me says he's going to *shoot* us if the guns aren't found... I don't think he's got the *nerve* personally... and I would advise you *not* to cough up!! The little *beast* wouldn't dare do anything and the old Brit. government ought to help a bit.' She little knew, I thought. 'So far they've been *politeness* itself, though I wouldn't say this place was the Ritz. The food's *awful*, all hot spices and Mexican wine and those awful tortillas they eat... but they've not *harmed* us and they're managing to be *polite*!!! They'd better *continue* to be, because if one of 'em comes too near he's likely to get a plate of tortillas in his face!!! It'll be nice to see you when this lot's over. Please don't let that *hot temper* of yours lead you into doing anything stupid... because you've got your career to think of and this was entirely *my* fault!!! Especially, don't get hurt. It would be *too awful* if I brought that on you. I'm all right... just *longing* to see you. Now I must stop because this horrid toad, Guzmán, is demanding the letter.'

On the back, Guzmán had written, 'Read and understood by Esplenderoso Benavenides Guzmán. The young lady is charming and obviously likes me already. I understand English.'

We searched the letter for clues to where she was, and I noticed that she'd put a dot under several of the letters. There were plenty of other dots about the page, of course, with the underlinings and exclamation marks, but I noticed that the dots under the letters spelled out Las Flores.

'Where's that?'

Nobody knew and I felt like weeping. Charley's letter was so brave and she'd taken quite a risk to give us some directions, and I stuffed it in my pocket with a lump in my throat. Charley had an awful knack of arousing the sentimental in me.

While Dan Tucker sent the Stutz back to his *hacienda* for half a dozen hands to join him, we prepared the cars, filling them with petrol, oil and water, checking the tyres and filling every available space with ammunition, food and maps and ten-gallon milk churns with spare petrol, water and oil for the crankcases.

Young Lukey, a lanky young man with enormous feet and huge dangling hands and a blond cowlick of hair over his eyes, found everything for us. He ran the garage but he was far less interested in cars than in motor-bikes, and anything we needed that he didn't possess such as food or ammunition, he provided by the simple means of jumping on to the ancient Moto-Rêve he owned and roaring up the street in a cloud of dust to demand it on our behalf.

'More Rêve than Moto at the moment,' he said with a grin. 'Got a wheel off a BSA and the tank off an Indian.'

He obviously adored the machine and talked about it incessantly as he assembled our needs, watched all the time by his grandfather who sat on a backless chair in the sun warming his old bones and muttering darkly about 'damn Yankees'.

One of the things he produced was a picture of Esplenderoso Guzmán. It had been taken on the International Bridge at El Paso when an American general had met Pancho Villa in 1914 to put the American point of view and try to curb his excesses. Guzmán was there among them and Lukey's spatulate oily finger rested on a tall handsome man who looked far more Spanish than Indian. He had a hatchet *hidalgo* face, an air of melancholy, a large moustache and fine dark eyes. His sombrero, its brim decorated with filigree, was well up on his head and his clothes, unlike Villa's and the others, looked immaculate and old-fashioned Mexican. The other men all seemed to be trying to emulate the Americans with their modern suits, but Guzmán had the look of a man who scorned modernity, and especially anything that smacked of America.

'Don't like Americans,' Lukey said. 'His brother was killed at Ojos Azules when the cavalry damn near caught Villa. Don't like the English either come to that.'

'Know anything else about him?' I asked.

'Some. He fell out with Villa because Villa wanted to fight the wars the modern way, with machine-guns and trains. He's a great guy for wrecking trains or using 'em to carry his army. Guzmán wanted it the old way – with horses and knives and a bit of old-fashioned gallantry.'

'Gallantry? Kidnapping a couple of girls?'

'I guess.' Lukey shrugged. 'Things is different now,' he said. 'He's a loser and in need of money. Huerta burned his house down in 1913 and Carranza destroyed a *hacienda* he had in Durango. He's desperate these days and they say that when he's removed Obregón he wants to go to Brazil or Argentina.'

'Who say?'

'The Mexes who come across the border to work tell us what he's up to.'

I frowned. 'I'll bet they also go back at night to say what *we're* up to,' I said.

All the same, it was a help to know something about Splendid Ben and to have an idea what he looked like. I had a feeling that if I ever met him I'd recognize him straight away.

–

We had the cars ready the next day and we stood back to check we had everything. They looked like the armoured vehicles Lawrence of Arabia had used in the desert against the Turks, every available inch packed with supplies, ammunition or weapons.

'Where Sheridan left off,' Tommy said grimly, 'Ford Motors take over.'

Half Camarillo turned out to see us off. Dan Tucker shook hands with us one after the other, followed a second later by Evalina who gave us enthusiastic kisses and told us to be careful. I noticed she lingered longer over Puddy than she did over me.

The Ford took a little starting so Tommy fished out a medicine dripper and dropped ether into the intake manifolds. Two cylinders caught, then all three, and in no time it was shuddering and shaking in what was supposed to be a gentle ticking-over. The Franklin was much easier. It started better and, because it had eight cylinders, its engine was smoother, turning over with a reassuring chunk-chunk-chunk.

We rolled out of Camarillo in a cloud of dust, Dan Tucker waiting for his men to arrive and Evalina jumping up and down with excitement and waving frantically to Puddy. As we rolled down to the river, Young Lukey accompanied us like an outrider, hurtling down one side of the little cavalcade and turning in front of us to hurtle back up the other, then round the back again to come up once more alongside and ahead.

We crossed the river in low gear, careful not to let water reach the ignition, and clunking and rattling across the rounded stones in the shallow stream. Young Lukey was still hurtling backwards and forwards in his enthusiasm, drenching himself and us in clouds of spray. Half the population of Camarillo employed servants from the Mexican side who crossed the stream every day by the ford, and the passage wasn't very difficult. With a farewell circle from Lukey, we started out on the road along which we'd not very long before returned.

After a while we passed the skeleton of Slingsby's horse, already stripped clean by vultures, then an abandoned sombrero, so we knew we were on the right track.

Soon afterwards, the wind started again, just as it had the first time, wailing from the west, filling our eyes and nostrils with grit. When we stopped to eat, it had grown so strong it was impossible to cook anything, so we made do with emergency rations that Captain O'Hara, of the cavalry, had supplied – pressed bars of a chocolate base mixed with dessicated vegetables and meat. We decided to continue after we'd eaten, but by this time the dust was so bad we had to put up the isinglass side curtains of the cars and pull the hoods down to avoid the worst of the weather. But then the wind threatened to take the hoods themselves away and the isinglass hissed continuously from the battering of the clouds of grit.

It was just beginning to grow dark when Tommy started banging on the Ford's klaxon and we came to a stop to allow them to catch up. But it wasn't the Ford which arrived, but the ranch hand called Snake-Eyes. What his real name was I never did find out, but he was certainly well-named because his eyes were slit-like, yellow and unblinking – even in the wind that was whipping grit into his face.

'Tom says it's a blown tyre,' he explained.

As he spoke, his hat was whipped off his head. He ran a few steps after it, realized he hadn't a cat in hell's chance of catching it and gave up the struggle.

We backed the Franklin down to the Ford rather than get out into the storm. Tommy had already jacked her up, unhitched the tyre and pulled out the tube. It had a horseshoe nail sticking into it. He tried to apply rubber solution to it but it was immediately covered with grit that made it useless and we decided instead to wait until daylight, left the cars where they were – nobody was likely to run into them after dark on a Mexican side road – and pitched an army tent among the rocks.

It was an uncomfortable night. In the shelter of the rocks, we managed to build a fire from the twigs of an *encino* tree, and as the wood flared and snapped we brewed coffee and cooked food out of tins, finally managing to get some sleep despite the flapping of the tent.

The following morning Tommy set about the tyre again. It took a long time but the wind had dropped and he hurriedly blew the rubber solution dry and slapped a patch on and we took it in turns to pump it up.

As we struggled into Acizpe del Oro, Mayor Gamboa was there again, glasses gleaming, popping up like a jack-in-a-box. 'First Chief Carranza has abandoned his attack on Veracruz,' he yelled. 'He has turned north again and is heading for Ciudad Juárez to raise the north against Obregón.'

'More likely the poor devil's been stopped from escaping by sea and he's taken to the hills,' Tommy said. 'It'll be Heaven help him if they catch him.'

Soon after leaving Acizpe, we reached the point where we'd had to turn back before. An old man was there with an ox-cart – in fact he looked like the same old man we'd seen before. Tommy questioned him closely but this time – if it *was* the same old man – he swore he'd not seen hide nor hair of Guzmán and his men and certainly not any *gringas señoritas* – foreign girls.

'I reckon one of Guzmán's boys has been at him,' Tommy growled.

We left the old man where he was and went on climbing. Though the wind had dropped a little, the sun seemed hotter than ever, and while the Franklin slogged doggedly upwards, the Ford began to cause trouble. The motormeter began to move from 'Good Average' to 'Higher Efficiency' and finally to 'Danger, Steaming'.

'Any minute now,' Tommy said, 'it'll be "Danger, Exploding". We've got to stop to let her get her breath back.'

We'd been driving too long in low gear. The Ford had overheated and the steam was screeching in the radiator, coming out in clouds from beneath the bonnet. It was half an hour before we could take the radiator cap off and considerably longer than that before we dare add the cold water from the cans.

When we started off again, the Ford was already misfiring. Tommy checked the coils and then the oil by opening the petcock with a pair of pliers. No oil ran out. There was none in the crankcase.

We filled it up again and set off once more. I was beginning to grow impatient by this time. With an aeroplane I could have done the job in half an hour, and here we were labouring along at the pace of a mule – an old mule. The Ford had been built for made-up asphalt roads, not this rocky track where the wheels wobbled constantly in the ruts or spun frantically as they churned up the deep dust until we all had to climb out of the Franklin and push. The gentle grades were almost too much for it and Tommy was constantly cleaning the timers and the spark plugs which persisted in oiling up. Every time we came to a steeper grade he had to turn round and reverse up it – because reverse was a lower gear – roaring and blowing off steam as he went.

'Mexico sure wasn't made for automobiles,' Snake-Eyes observed wryly.

We'd stopped because the Ford's cylinder block was overheating now and Tommy was frightened the pistons would set solid in the cylinders. And finally we knew, as it grew dark at the end of the day, that there'd be no further forward movement because you needed high speed to keep the Ford's head-lights bright. Unlike the Franklin, which took current from a battery, the Ford used current direct from the flywheel and it was impossible to get up enough speed on the bad ground.

By the following morning, I knew we were beaten once more. The Ford's oil line was clogged and Tommy had to unscrew the radiator to uncover the timing gear. Clearing the oil line with the tyre pump, we carefully put it all back again, but it seemed to take hours. Then, having refilled the radiator, we checked the crankcase again before setting off, and discovered it was once more as dry as a bone.

We filled it up with the last of the oil, knowing perfectly well we were at the end of our tether. I was growing more and more jumpy, and more and more angry with the whole affair. Every time I thought of Charley in her grubby prison I wanted to explode. But I held on to my temper because an idea was growing in my mind, and the more I thought about it the stronger it grew.

The Ford had devoured almost all our oil now, while the Franklin swallowed petrol as fast as we could put it in the tank. I was also beginning to grow worried about the way the big car was behaving. The road showed no signs of improving and, as it constantly wound upwards between the rocks and *mesquite*, even the Franklin was growing hot because we were moving so slowly. The sun seemed to blaze down and the wind had dropped completely, leaving us in a furnace-like atmosphere that caught at the breath and left us panting and our clothes saturated with sweat.

Finally we heard the clunk-clunk of a burned-out bearing and knew it was the end of the road for the Ford. Tommy, his face damp with sweat and coated with the yellow dust that had stuck to it, looked at me agonizedly. I knew he felt he'd failed me, that somehow he ought to have done better.

'I guess we'll have to leave her here,' he said.

'Them Mexes'll pinch it chop-chop, Mister Tom,' Archie pointed out.

'Then they'll have to damn well pinch it,' Tommy said. 'I'm sick of it.'

'It's four hundred dollars, Boss.'

'We can afford four hundred dollars.'

Archie looked at him sideways, as if he might offer to carry the Ford back to Camarillo on his own shoulders if he could have the four hundred dollars.

'We'll all have to crowd into the Franklin,' Tommy said.

'How?' Slingsby asked. 'Six men, oil, water, petrol, supplies and enough damned guns and ammunition to start a war.'

'That's what we came for, isn't it?' Tommy snapped. 'To start a war.'

'What happens if the Franklin conks?' Slingsby persisted. 'Then there'll be six men and a lot of ammunition stranded God knows how many miles inside Mexico. It'd be a long walk back.'

'We've got to do *something*.'

'Shapin' up the way we are,' Slingsby insisted, 'we aren't going to do so damn much.'

Somehow Slingsby seemed to have divined what was taking shape in my mind. 'We've got to go back,' he insisted.

'After we've come so far?'

'If we go on, we'll arrive dead beat and probably end up prisoners, too.'

It made sense and Tommy knew it.

We pushed the Ford off the road and turned the Franklin round – not without difficulty because it was a huge vehicle and the road was narrow. But we did it in the end and set off down the hill. There was no labouring engine going this way and I let the big vehicle coast down under its own weight. Tommy sat glumly in the back, staring blankly in front of him, clearly obsessed by a feeling of failure. Puddy sat alongside him, crammed in with the two ranch hands and the weapons, smoking, holding his cigarette back to front. The two ranch hands seemed to be thinking chiefly of their next meal.

We'd dumped all the gear for the Ford, and if someone found it who knew something about cars, he was going to do well out of it. We'd also dumped all the unnecessary water and kept only enough petrol to get us back to the border. Slingsby, sitting in the front next to me, looked surprisingly bright under the coating of dust on his face. He said nothing but he kept glancing at me and I knew he was certain now of what I'd decided.

We reached the bottom of the slope, ran on to the plain that led to the river in half the time it had taken us to climb away from it, and roared into Acizpe del Oro, expecting to refill with oil, water and petrol, have a meal and doubtless learn the latest on Carranza from Jesús Gregorio Gamboa, the Mayor. But this time it was different. Almost before we knew where we were, we found ourselves among a mass of mounted men who surrounded the car immediately.

'*Alto!*'

As we pulled to a stop I found myself staring at a circle of rifle muzzles. The owners were an ugly lot with their fierce black eyes and moustaches, but they were colourful, too, with gold badges on sombreros and jackets, and brilliant *rebozos*, gaudy kerchiefs and tiger-striped *sarapes* vivid against the theatrical faded pinks, greens and mauves of the town walls. There was a reek of horseflesh, sweat and gun oil about them and a strong sense of menace that didn't come just from the guns. Lean men on leaner horses, some with bare bronze feet wearing a single spur, carrying carbines and slung about with cartridge belts, milled about us, then a tall man in breeches and boy scout hat with a bushy moustache pushed his horse forward and cocked a revolver.

'Out,' he said in English.

I was seething with fury and frustration, because I'd begun to get some constructive ideas, and this wasn't the time to be kidnapped ourselves. But, staring into the muzzles of about twenty rifles, there wasn't much we could do, and we had no real right to be there. As I climbed to the dusty road, I heard the crash of a volley of musketry from behind the houses and a yell of triumph. The man in the boy scout hat grinned.

'Carrancistas,' he said. 'We are shooting them. We do not like First Chief Carranza.'

Slingsby looked startled, then as though he'd like to punch someone in the jaw. Tommy grabbed his arm.

'Hold it, Sling,' he said. 'Those Carrancistas are probably lucky. This lot are Villa's men and at least it's quick, because they have a few other ways of sending a guy to his Maker – smeared with molasses and staked out over an ants' nest; sewn up in wet hides that shrink in the sun and suffocate; strung out over a quick-growing cactus so that it shoves its spike through you as it grows.'

The Mexicans were shouting and singing a ribald ditty about what villains they were – '*Todos los alzados, y los forjidos, y los dediciosos*' – then I saw a car that had been shot up, dripping blood like a slaughtered bull. It contained two or three corpses and, as more yelling came from further down the street, I saw a group of armed men dragging the Mayor from his office, together with half his male relations and two or three of his council. Gamboa's smile had gone, and he was weeping and pleading. As he stood with his hands together, begging for mercy, a big man on a black horse, a huge high-spirited animal which he mastered as if he were part of it, rode up, reached from the saddle to unhook the framed portrait of Carranza from alongside the Mayor's door and smashed it down over the Mayor's head. The Mayor staggered back against the wall, his spectacles crooked, the picture round his shoulders like a huge square collar. Pieces of glass were sticking in his cheeks and his eyes rolled with pain and terror. The rider sat back in the massive silver-embossed Mexican saddle and grinned.

'Who's the big ape?' Slingsby growled.

'Dry up, bud,' Snake-Eyes muttered. 'That's Pancho Villa.'

'Himself?'

'Himself.'

The thought that we'd come face to face with the legendary bandit-patriot took my breath away. Villa was supposed to detest the British and the Americans and it was a jarring thought that he might enjoy, in his twisted cruelty, wreaking some vengeance on us for trespassing on Mexican soil, just when we were needed. Poor old Charley, I thought. She was going to have to wait a little longer – perhaps a *lot* longer.

The Mexicans were dragging the Mayor and his friends down the street now, the Mayor still wearing the picture round his neck like some tragi-comic character from a play. He could hardly stand up and the soldiers were shoving him from one to another so that he staggered constantly from side to side. Finally disappearing round a corner, once more there was that sickening crash of a volley of musketry, and I knew it was Gamboa's death knell.

There were yells of '*Viva Villa*', and I saw the rider of the black horse had jumped from the saddle now and was walking towards us. He was a man of medium height but powerfully built with the short bowed legs and pigeon toes of a life-long horseman. He had a big moustache, reddish-brown kinky hair, and a perpetually open mouth as if he had adenoids. He wore a yellow leather *charro* suit, a *peso*-studded sombrero, jingling spurs and a *sarape*, and the extra Indio finery of a scarf and a vermilion sash.

He stopped in front of me and stared at me with steady topaz eyes, his hands on his gun belt. There was a long silence and I was just wondering what he intended to do with us, when he swept off his sombrero to hold it to his chest, grinned and stuck out his hand.

'*Señor Commandante Falcoñair! Salud!*'

He spoke my name in the Spanish manner and the man in the scout hat grinned.

'Pancho Villa offers greetings.'

This was a bit unexpected, to say the least. Uneasily, I took Villa's hand and felt my fingers crunch in his great grip. Then he spoke rapidly in Spanish again and the man in the scout hat translated. 'Pancho Villa presents his greetings and says welcome. He hopes you will take wine and talk with him.'

I glanced at Tommy and he shrugged. Slingsby was scowling, while Puddy, I noticed, having seen this sort of murderous behaviour in his native Russia, was staring coldly at the Mexicans. Since we seemed to have no alternative, I nodded.

'Tell him I will,' I said. 'But tell him I want a guard on the motor car.'

'*Mí jefe—*'

The man in the scout hat rattled away in quick Spanish and Villa grinned and jabbered back.

'Pancho Villa says there will be a guard and when you return there will be nothing missing. If anyone so much as touches anything, he will be shot at once.'

'It's nice to know.'

'It's nicer still,' Archie observed, 'to know we're going to *come* back.'

Villa swaggered off up the street and the man in the scout hat nudged us to follow. Further along, there was a gap in the houses and against a bare *adobe* wall pocked with bullet holes, I saw several bodies. Among them was Gamboa, whom I recognized from the sash he was wearing and the picture frame round his neck. He had fallen backwards and the big wooden frame had propped him up in a curiously living fashion, his mouth gaping, his smashed spectacles still on his nose, his face covered with blood.

We tried hard not to look. Since 1910 Mexico had been drenched in blood; and assassinations, firing parties, hangings, senseless butchery and mindless, medieval cruelty against the families and officials of absentee landlords and politicians had become part of the daily scene. It was horrifying and hateful, but it was not our affair, and I suspected that any comment on our part would probably have put us against a wall ourselves. Our job was to save Charley not get involved in the tortuous byways of Mexican politics.

Not far along the street was what passed for a *cantina*. Its name – Las Puertas Celestiales, the Heavenly Gates – was painted in square-ended Victorian lettering on a lopsided board over the entrance. It was a flat-faced building with saloon doors, and outside was a verandah surrounded by flowers, vines and dusty pot plants.

Villa pulled forward a table with cast-iron legs and a marble top and gestured us to chairs. Wine and *tequila* appeared – though I noticed Villa didn't touch it – followed by a meal on earthenware plates of chicken, corn, *garbanzos*, *tortillas* and *frijoles*, with a great *olla* of cool water, a bowl of goatsmilk cheese and a dish of chilli sauce.

'It isn't much,' the interpreter said. 'But the Chief says you are welcome. He wishes to know if you need petrol or oil.'

'Tell him yes,' Tommy said.

We were all a little puzzled by this time, and Dan Tucker's two ranch hands were plain scared and not afraid to show it. Knowing that Villa's dislike of Americans and Europeans came from the hatred of Indians and Mestizos oppressed for centuries by the Spaniards and their descendants, I couldn't imagine we were there just to pass the time of day.

It was one of the weirdest meals I've ever eaten. We sat at the marble-topped table while a frightened girl served us. All round us, watching us, were Villa's Dorados – his Golden Boys, the men of his personal bodyguard recognizable by the badges on their sombreros. They'd paused in their butchery of the Carrancistas in Acizpe to watch us eat, and to one side a grinning soldier twanged on a guitar and sang.

Si Carranza se casa con Villa,
Y Zapata con General Obregón,
Si Adelita se casa conmigo,
Pos se acabará la revolución.

A burly sphinx, Villa sat silently watching, but he grinned as the guitarist was joined by a mouth organist and they started to play *The Fight at Fresno* and *Pancho Villa's Wedding* and the ribald revolutionary *La Cucaracha*, all marching songs his troops had acquired in the ten years of fighting.

The meal was rough but it was welcome, and as we ate Villa quietly smoked a thin Mexican cigar. Then, suddenly he started to make a long speech which seemed to be addressed to me. The man in the scout hat translated.

'Pancho Villa presents his compliments and hopes you have enjoyed his proffered hospitality. He now wishes to talk business.'

'What about?' Tommy asked in Spanish. So far he'd used only English for safety but now, as they discovered he could understand their language, the discussion became more lively.

'He's heard of you, Brat,' Tommy said. 'He's read of you in *El Heralde del Norte* – that's a newspaper that circulates in Chihuahua. I expect some *muchacho* in Camarillo found out about you and passed the information over the border. He says you're a *gran caballero* – that's a gallant knight – and he's proud to meet you. He knows you're a very brave man, and he knows you have many decorations for courage and have fought in the skies all over Europe. He wants – hold your hat on – he wonders if you'd be prepared to organize an air force and lead it.'

'For him?'

'That's what he says. He knows there are aeroplanes for sale and he wonders if he can buy two or three?'

'Strewth,' Slingsby said.

This was a startler and no mistake. I was in Mexico not to start an air force for a bandit chief but to rescue Charley.

'He'll make you a general,' Tommy continued, 'and if we join him, the rest of us'll all become colonels. It looks to me, Brat, as if your fame's arrived ahead of you. He says he thinks it'll be impossible to overthrow Obregón unless he modernizes his army. He's already learned how to use motor cars and trains to make war, and he feels it's time to learn to use aeroplanes.'

Villa grinned, nodded and gestured at the rifles held by his men. There were Winchesters, Mausers, Remingtons, Krags, Sharps, Mannlichers, Colts, Lebels, Springfields, Mondragóns, even old Martini-Henrys and a few more I couldn't recognize.

'He says that if only one rifle and one calibre bullet had been invented, he could have taken Mexico in ninety days. His constant worry was getting the right ammunition for his weapons.'

Villa leaned forward and spoke again to the man in the scout hat.

'*Sí, mi capitán!*' Scout Hat turned to me. 'The Great Captain says that one day we shall have in Mexico a "*Republica de los Indios*—"'

'A republic of Mexicans, he means,' Tommy said. 'Without Spanish or European influence.'

'*No hago ronda con chocolateros*,' Villa growled and Tommy explained.

'He says he's got no time for chocolate-drinkers. He means foreigners and city-dwellers.'

Scout Hat nodded and smiled. 'He says he knows that the British supported the usurper, Huerta, against Madero, whom he loved, and he says that he could finish Obregón, who executes the destitute for stealing a loaf while he allows his friends, who have made fortunes from corruption, to ride around in automobiles. He wishes you to be his good friend and to lead his air force.'

'Not damn likely,' I murmured. 'Tommy, tell him no.'

'Dress it up a bit, though, Boss,' Archie added quickly. 'It'll pay.'

'Tell him we're still British officers,' I went on. 'Puddy, too. And we could be court-martialled and shot if we help him.'

'We'll probably be court-martialled and shot if we don't,' Slingsby murmured. 'By *him*.'

Tommy took a long time to put the matter across and I knew he was toning my reply down a bit. Villa frowned, then he shook his head.

'*Y al reresarme me iba bebienda las lágrimas más amargas de mí vida*,' he said.

'He says he's drinking the bitterest tears of his life,' Tommy translated, and Villa went off again. 'He says when he first came out in support of Madero, he had great hopes for the people of Mexico and had great visions painted on his heart. He says the raid on Camarillo was not his doing, nor was – and it's news to me! – the raid on Columbus. He says he should never have allowed Madero to be murdered. He should have foreseen it. He committed a black infamy – *una negra infamia* – and his heart is between two stones.'

Villa scowled and rattled off in Spanish again.

'He explains,' Tommy went on, 'that, unlike all the others, he's got nothing from the revolution – which is exactly what he asked for – and that his heart bleeds for the confusion of his people.'

'Tell him I'm sorry but the answer's still no.'

Villa frowned and spoke again. 'He says,' Tommy translated, 'that once it was land and freedom, now it's land and the dark. They have reached the shadows. It's all over. His men are tired and so is he. Since you can't help him, he's going to head for Sabinas in Coahuila.'

'*Un golpe terrifico*,' Villa snapped.

'He'll capture it in his usual way – by a terrific blow – and then he'll pull up the railway track on either side so he can't be surprised, telegraph Mexico City and offer to lay down his arms in return for a ranch and a pension. He understands that your loyalty lies with our own king, and he begs you when you next meet him to give him the regards of Pancho Villa. He understands the way you feel and admires you for it because he admires courage and forthrightness, and Mexico has been a mesh of treachery for too long. He says we can go.'

Tommy drew a deep breath and Villa stood up. He gestured towards the Franklin and, as we began to walk back to it, he spoke to the man in the scout hat.

'He says he knows we are seeking Guzmán,' the interpreter said. 'He says he hopes you find him because he has nothing but hatred and contempt in his heart for such men. Guzmán is a *gachupín* – a descendant of a Spaniard – and, despite the friendship that once existed between them, he has shown only treachery and he needs to be hanged. If he can he'll send word to you somehow, where Guzmán is, and if it's ever possible will even help you, so long as it doesn't stop his attack on Sabinas.'

–

We drove out of Acizpe faintly dazed, Archie and Snake-Eyes clearly very relieved. Villa rode alongside the car for a hundred yards or so, his spurs a-jingle, like some centaur, smiling and talking incessantly. On the edge of the town there were a few trees and from the branches dangled grotesque groups of newly hanged men, like bunches of grapes.

The Mexicans didn't even bother to look at them and I remembered the strange Mexican preoccupation with death I'd read about. They always seemed to be talking about it: they even had a Festival of Death every year, when people dressed up as corpses and the children ate little cakes decorated with skeletons. Even men about to be shot accepted death as inevitable and squabbled over a cigarette before turning politely to the firing squad that would topple them into newly-dug graves.

Scout Hat saw me frowning at the corpses. 'Carrancistas,' he explained. 'Carranza's general, Murguía, hanged our people in the same way in Chihuahua City in 1917 – two hundred and fifty-six of them. He said they weren't worth a bullet and the place is still known as the Avenue of the Hanging Men.'

As we passed the last grisly group of swaying bodies, Villa took off his sombrero, waved it and turned away. The other horsemen turned to him, letting off their rifles into the air and shouting '*Viva Falcoñair*', '*Viva Villa*' and '*El Ilustre Panchito*'. As we headed out into the countryside again, Tommy drew a deep, deep breath that seemed to come up from his boots.

'Phew,' he said. 'And thank the Lord!'

Snake-Eyes gestured. 'And then some,' he said.

Chapter 5

Tommy's father was waiting near the river with five of his hands, all well mounted and armed.

'Where are the girls?' he said.

Tommy scowled. 'That damned Ford,' he said. 'I guess we need something bigger than a Ford.'

'Didn't you get to the girls?'

'Never saw 'em,' Archie growled. 'And we darned near got ourselves hung by Villa.'

Tucker's jaw dropped. 'Villa? You ran into Villa?'

'You're darned tootin' we did, boss. My neck was sure feeling ticklish all the time that talking was going on.'

'What happened?'

'He wanted an air force.'

Tommy explained and old Tucker frowned. 'You can reckon yourselves lucky,' he said. 'What about the girls?'

'We haven't found them,' Tommy growled. 'We couldn't go on. We've got to think this one out.'

Slingsby glanced at me. 'I think we've thought it out,' he said.

Tommy's head jerked up and the jaded look vanished at once. 'We have?'

'Sure we have.'

Slingsby looked again at me and I gestured. 'I don't know why we didn't think of it before,' I said. 'It was there right under our noses and we didn't see it. We can do this job in an hour with a bit of luck.'

'How?'

Tommy stared, then the light dawned on him. He glanced at Puddy and *he* saw daylight too.

'Aeroplanes!'

'*You* said it,' I pointed out. 'A couple of days ago. We're aviators. Let's aviate.'

–

'But where the blazes are we going to get aeroplanes?' Tommy asked.

Back in Camarillo, they'd got the place more or less back to shape. Dust had been kicked over the blood the dead Mexicans had left behind after the raid, the holed bus had been towed away to Lukey's garage for repairs, and the charred back half of the hotel was being pulled down by men with axes, saws, ropes and teams of horses. The store was just a pile of ashes and charred wood through which the proprietor and his family were picking for anything that could still be sold, even at half-price.

Captain O'Hara had posted his men along the river bank. He'd set up posts and they'd strung up a couple of strands of barbed wire and were sitting behind them with their horses and tents, knowing that the Mexicans couldn't gallop across again as they pleased. The barbed wire didn't seem very strong compared with what we'd seen on the Western Front in France, but it wasn't intended to withstand artillery or attacks at brigade level, and it was certainly strong enough to withstand a few Mexicans on horses excited by *tequila*.

Then Emiliano Ojarra turned up – as Irish as O'Hara himself. Despite his black hair, he had merry grey eyes instead of the usual jetty orbs, a blunt nose as tip-tilted as the Captain's, a healthy round red face and a jutting chin. He looked as much an Irishman as Captain O'Hara, who seemed already to have accepted that they came originally from the same Irish bog.

Ojarra was an educated man. When the revolution had started in 1910, by skill and hard work he'd managed to acquire land. Since retiring from the war, he'd increased his boundaries by buying land belonging to men beggared by the revolution. Now he was wealthy and influential, and clearly a great friend of Dan Tucker's. He had no love for Esplenderoso Guzmán and was only too willing to help. And, what was even better, he thought he knew where Guzmán would have holed out.

'How'd you find out?'

'Pancho Villa and I,' he explained in excellent English, 'have never quarrelled.'

'Villa told you?'

'Not Villa himself. But I heard a whisper from Acizpe del Oro. There is a ruined *hacienda*. A place called Las Flores.'

'That's what Charley's letter said.'

'It belonged to a *gachupín* called José Ynez Renterías who owned the land round it.' Ojarra gestured towards the border and the hills rising beyond them. 'It's in the hills. He was a good man and he looked after his *peóns*. But it didn't stop him being murdered when the revolution started and nailed to his own front door.'

'Charmin',' Slingsby commented.

'Guzmán is from Mexico City,' Ojarra went on. 'He's educated and came out for Madero in 1910. He didn't kill for the sake of killing and didn't ill-treat his prisoners then, but he's changed now and no one knows what he might do. They say he's become a little mad.'

'Where's the *hacienda*?'

'A hundred and fifty kilometres inside Mexico. Eighty miles.'

'Eighty miles! Show me where?'

A map was brought and Ojarra jabbed a finger at the brown shading that indicated the hills. 'I know the place. I have visited it in the days of José Ynez Renterías, who was a friend of mine.'

At least we now knew where Charley and the French girl were.

Knowing nothing about aeroplanes, however, neither Ojarra, nor Captain O'Hara nor Tommy's father were able to help much. They listened to the discussion with the blank eyes of people for whom it was way above their heads. We were all sitting in a corner of the hotel saloon with the Sheriff; despite prohibition, the proprietor had produced Mexican beer, a great deal of which had been needed to slake our thirsts.

Though Tommy liked the idea of flying, he was still digging out the bugs in the idea. 'Where do we get the aeroplanes?' he repeated, and I guessed he hadn't really quite got his breath back from that meeting with Villa. 'This isn't New York or Washington. They're not made in Camarillo and nobody round here's got one.'

'There's somebody round San José's got one,' I pointed out.

‘Who?’

‘The widow of that chap Matthews, who killed himself. She had a De Havilland and an Avro. I gathered they weren’t in much of a shape and I dare bet nobody’s been rushing to buy ’em. She’s probably desperate for money and will be glad to get rid of ’em. It was my impression she wasn’t particularly enamoured of flying, anyway, and would be happy to go back to a normal life. We could tune ’em up between us and have ’em down to Camarillo in an afternoon. We could then fly over this Las Flores place and pick ourselves a landing-ground – a matter of an hour, there and back – then we can decide how to set about getting the girls to safety.’

The idea obviously appealed and Tommy’s face began to lighten.

‘How much do you reckon she’d want for the buses?’ he said.

‘She’d probably give ’em to you if you offered ’em a good home and her train fare to wherever she wants to go.’

Dan Tucker shook his head. ‘We’d make it worth her while,’ he insisted. ‘I wouldn’t want her to come out of it badly and, dammit, we can afford it.’

‘The almighty dollar speaking,’ Tommy grinned.

‘Well, hell, son—’

'It's all right, Pa. I'm only teasing. It's a noble sentiment.' Tommy swung round to me. 'I've never flown a DH.'

'I have. They're like any other bus.'

'What about repairs? If it's not in the best of health, it's going to need some.'

'We can rig it. We know enough about it. And we can tune the engine. We'd need a bit of expertise on patching the wings and a carpenter to repair cracked struts.'

'We've got one,' Tommy said. 'On the ranch. A smithy, too. And women who can sew. They'll have those wings looking like last-century samplers if you want 'em that way!'

Dan Tucker seemed to be growing impatient. 'Then, for the good Lord's sake,' he said, 'when y'all have finished yacking, let's go get them aeroplanes!'

–

Leaving Archie and Snake-Eyes to find a landing-field under the guidance of Slingsby and Young Lukey, the rest of us crowded into the Franklin and set off back towards Marfa. We did it in record time and just managed to catch the train as it pulled out. Hiring a taxi as we arrived in San José, we drove straight out to the airfield.

All the flags and ribbons that had been fluttering on the day we'd flown the Jenny were still there, but they had a curiously neglected look now. Mamie Matthews was sitting on a box with the mechanic, Red, apparently the only one in the whole circus prepared to stand by her. All the others – the man in the hard straw hat who'd sold the tickets, the labourers who'd swung the aeroplanes into wind, the band, the man who'd sold hot dogs – had all vanished. All that was left were half a dozen packing cases, a carpet bag which seemed to contain all Mrs Matthews's possessions, a Ford with part of its tonneau converted into a truck body, and two old aeroplanes, only one of which, the Avro, was at the moment visible.

When I looked at it again, my heart sank. It was in far worse condition than I'd remembered – much worse than the Jenny we'd flown, and *that* had killed Matthews. But we weren't intending to do any stunts – just a simple up and down, and back again. And, unlike Matthews, we were all experienced pilots unlikely to take risks. With a little effort, I decided, we might still be able to do it, though I didn't like the look of the binding of wire and sticky tape round the propeller.

'It touched the ground once as he came in,' Mamie Matthews said. 'He taught himself to fly, you see.'

'Taught *himself*?' Tommy said.

It didn't surprise me. Plenty of people in the early days had taken aeroplanes up with nothing more than a few chats with a pilot, something that had been quite possible in the days of Caudrons and Farmans, even if it no longer was; the Avro had bridged the gap between the old and the new, arriving after the Farmans but before the newer, faster, trickier machines. She was a straightforward, well-designed aeroplane and air-mad young men all over America and England, who'd flown in the war and couldn't give it up, were using them for their little circuses. They stunted well and were easy to land, and they were handy on the controls with no vices or idiosyncrasies. There was even an apocryphal story of an officer who'd swung the propeller and, before he could climb aboard, had seen his machine shoot off down the field and lift itself into the air. Following it for miles in a car, he'd finally caught it up just in time to see it land itself, empty of petrol, and come to rest quietly and without fuss. That was how stable the Avro was.

The only thing likely to upset anybody who hadn't flown one was the rotary engine. It was an eighty-horse Monosoupape; like all rotaries, it had a fixed crankshaft round which the cylinders spun. It had only two speeds – on, when it was running full bore, and off, when it was stopped – and it required a little skill to handle.

'How about that prop, though?' Tommy asked.

'We got another,' Red said. 'In that there crate.'

He started the engine for us and, as it went off with a crackling roar, I taxied the machine round the field once or twice and even tried lifting the wheels off the ground. It was far from perfect but I thought it would do the trick.

I climbed out and Tommy looked at me as I tried to flatten my hair, which had been stiffened by the slipstream. I nodded and he turned to the mechanic.

'Want a job?' he asked.

Red indicated Mamie who was still sitting disconsolately on a crate.

'I got one,' he said. 'I'll stick with Mamie.'

'It's only for a month,' Tommy pointed out.

'That all?'

'Sure is. And the pay's good. I want you just long enough to set her up and make sure she flies. It'll take only a day or two, I guess, but I'll take you on for a month for safety.'

Red looked at Mamie. 'Okay,' he said. 'I'll see to it. She'll fly when I've finished with her.'

'I want her in Camarillo tomorrow.'

The mechanic stared. 'You ain't asking much,' he said.

'That's why the pay's good,' Tommy explained. He indicated me and Puddy. 'You've got plenty of help. We'll fix up lights and work through the night. Tomorrow we'll fly her down. The crates can follow in the truck.'

Red looked at Mrs Matthews, then he nodded. 'Done,' he said. 'When do we start?'

'We haven't finished yet,' I pointed out. 'We need *two* machines.'

'Two?' Tommy's jaw dropped.

'We can't fetch off one girl and then go back for the other.'

'People have clung to wings before long enough to lift 'em to safety!'

'Who's going to cling to the wings? One of the girls?'

'Hell, no!' Tommy looked flustered. He was very much the Southern gentleman and, despite Evalina, who could ride, shoot and even handle cattle, he still treated girls as if they were made of porcelain and wore the roses and crinolines of the Old South. 'I wouldn't expect *that*.'

'Well, if one of *us* clings to the wings,' I said, 'who's going to fly the aeroplane? The girls can't.'

'Can't we cram 'em both in the cockpit?'

'How do we know how long the field we're going to have to use is? If it's short, we'd never get off, with three up.'

'It might *not* be short.'

'We don't know. And if it *is*, we won't have a second chance. We've got to be prepared to do it in one go if we have to.'

'Okay,' he said. He turned to Red. 'We'll have the DH as well. Where is it??'

The mechanic peeled himself a stick of chewing gum and cocked a thumb at the barn which had been Matthew's undoing. It was still minus a lot of tiles and was scorched at the end.

'She's in there,' he said.

'Why?'

'Won't fly.'

'Why not?'

'Motor needs tuning.'

'I reckon we can handle that,' I said. 'I'll get her up if the engine works.'

Red glanced at Mrs Matthews and grinned suddenly. 'You'll be right clever, son, if you do. She ain't got no wings on her.'

I frowned, wondering if he were just enjoying toying with me because I was young and had a different accent from him.

'Have you got the wings?' I asked.

'Sure have.'

'How long will it take to put 'em on?'

'A long time, Mister. Clint taxied her into another Jenny we had. The Jenny was a write-off. It didn't do the DH's wings much good.'

'How long?' I asked once more.

He glanced again at Mrs Matthews and scratched his head. 'They sure need some carpentering doing on 'em,' he said.

'How about the wheels?' Tommy asked. 'Can we tow her out to my place?'

'I guess so.'

'Well we've got the carpenters, and we've got sewing machines for saddlery. I guess they'll do what we need. I'll take her.'

The mechanic and Mrs Matthews stared at each other. They looked as if they couldn't believe their ears.

'You'll buy 'em?' Mrs Matthews asked.

'At a fair price.'

She shrugged. 'I guess I don't know what a fair price would be,' she admitted. 'Not much, I reckon. Not if you've got to tune 'em up, repair 'em and rig 'em yourself.'

'I'll leave you to work it out,' Tommy said. 'My lawyers will make sure we don't pay too much and *I'll* see we don't pay too little.' He fished in his wallet and put two one-hundred-dollar bills on the crate. 'That's a deposit.'

Mrs Matthews stared at them as if they were manna from heaven. It was my impression that in the Great Flying Circus she'd never seen much more than a few crumpled dollar bills at a time. Judging by her possessions, they'd probably lived a hand-to-mouth existence and even left debts behind them all over the country.

'Okay,' she said. She picked up the two bills and stared at them. 'I'll be able to go home and see my folks,' she said. 'I haven't been home since I married Clint.'

–

We arranged to hire the barn from the owner of the field. As he moved out bales of hay and old farming equipment, we pushed the Avro inside alongside the DH. Already Red was fixing up a cluster of lights from the roof, hanging them on wires over the beams so we could work all night if necessary. I didn't intend to fly over the rugged Mexican territory without being certain that the machine would get me back in one piece.

I owed so much by this time to Tommy, I tried to tell him that I'd try to pay him back when I got the chance, but he brushed the offer aside.

'Forget it,' he said. 'If it comes off, it'll make a good story for the newspapers and the Old Man'll make sure they know. He's one of the old timers, but he's got a reputation for doing rugged things and he'll love it. Besides, it won't do any harm in other ways. Americans like the pioneer spirit and this sort of publicity'll encourage people to do business with him.'

Mamie Matthews had already disappeared to the station – I doubted if Red would ever see her again – and we started immediately by taking off the propeller. Puddy and I hoisted it clear and lifted the new brass-tipped one from the crate into its place. There were plenty of gashes in the fuselage and wings but, with Red's assistance, we bought fresh Irish linen in the town and patched them, sewing them in place by hand, then gluing them and doping them down. During the night, helped by me, Red went through the engine with a tooth comb, putting aside tinfuls of nuts, bolts, washers, screws and parts, until the barn stank of dope, petrol and oil, and stale coffee made on a kerosene stove lent to us by the farmer's wife. The farmer's children had moved in early and a row of heads over one of the stalls had watched wide-eyed until bedtime.

Meanwhile Tommy and Puddy were examining the DH. 'We can repair it,' Tommy announced. 'The engine's a Liberty. Four hundred horse. Big enough to lift anything, with cylinders like beer barrels. Wings are in a mess – the usual spruce frame, mind – and they'll have to be glued and tacked and screwed in places. But hell, at the ranch we've got plenty of help. We can have 'em repaired as quickly as it takes the glue and the dope to dry. Rigging 'em'll take another day, then we can brace 'em and away we go.'

'You have to lay the tape over every rib,' I pointed out earnestly, 'and work round the edges, using the right number of stitches to the inch and locking 'em where necessary.'

'I've seen wings repaired,' Tommy said indignantly. 'We all have. While one of us is finding out just where this damn Hacienda Las Flores is, the rest of us can be getting the DH airworthy. How long do you think we've got?'

'Three or four days.'

I saw Red's jaw drop. Tommy stared. 'Three or four days?' he said.

'We've got to do a recce to find this place, and when we've found it we've got to go straight in and fetch the girls out. No nonsense. If we delay, they'll move 'em further away. We'll be flying down to Camarillo tomorrow morning and doing the recce over the border in the afternoon. We'll need the DH rigged and ready the next day or the day after.'

Tommy looked startled. 'We've got a lot to do!' he said. 'The wings are dihedral, and the angle's got to be exact. We'll need to work with an inclinometer.'

'We've got one,' Red said.

'It'll mean wedges and sheerings,' Tommy went on. 'We've got to rig for a fore-and-aft angle as well, and we've got to check the centre section panel, to say nothing of the struts, longerons, turtleback, fin, elevator and rudder. Strewth, there's a lot to do there, Brat!'

'Three or four days,' I said.

Tommy sighed. 'Okay,' he said. 'We'll do it. Somehow.'

Red was screwing the drip pan and the cowling back in place. He looked exhausted as I walked round the Avro, frowning, touching the rudder and the ailerons and kicking the tyres.

'Who's going to do the recce?' Tommy asked.

'I am.'

'We ought to draw lots.'

'No,' I insisted. 'Charley's my responsibility and I've had more experience than anybody else.'

'How are we going to do it?' Tommy looked worried. 'They'll be off as soon as they see us landing.'

'I've thought of that,' I said. 'There's Ojarra. He'll help.'

–

The Avro was ready by dawn, and, wheeling it out in the grey light, I climbed into the pilot's seat, dressed just as I was, without flying coat, helmet or goggles. Normally the pilot's seat was the rear one but to make things easier for passengers, it had been changed to the front. Surrounded as I was by the centre section and the wings, and the characteristic skid – like a big ski between the wheels – hardly made the machine look sleek.

I sniffed the air and looked round me. Tommy and Puddy were watching anxiously, and I saw Red screwing at his flat cap.

I turned on the petrol and opened the throttle needle valve which supplied juice to the crankcase. As I waved, Red spun the propeller to push the petrol vapour into the cylinders where it combined with the air drawn in through the suction valve on the cylinder head. This valve was uncontrolled, just sucking air as the piston moved down, and the resultant mixture was explosive only if the correct amount of vapour had reached the cylinder. And this, as I well knew, was designed to work only when the motor was running flat out.

'Contact!'

I switched on, and Tommy heaved on the propeller. There was a roar as the engine caught and the slipstream began to blast at my cheeks round the stubby windscreen. Switching the engine on and off with the cut-out switch, a bell-push sort of affair on the top of the mahogany joystick, I waved away the chocks. As Puddy and Red heaved at the ropes, I allowed the engine to roar to move the machine ahead, then blipped the switch once more, cutting the engine again and again as I edged forward, because that was the only way to keep a rotary running until you were ready. If you paused too long, sheets of flame from the ejected petrol were inclined to envelope the engine and cowling.

There was no time to fiddle about or make checks and I'd done them all beforehand; once a rotary engine caught, you were on your way. Putting the rudder hard over, I allowed the engine to swing the tail round. Cutting the engine, I reversed rudder and allowed the engine to roar again until I was straight and began to move down the field, then I swung her into the wind and took my thumb off the button.

Freed from any restraint, the Mono howled and the machine rattled and bumped down the field, the slipstream flattening the grass. As I lifted off the ground, I could see Puddy, Tommy and Red the mechanic, standing in a line outside the barn, watching me.

I let her gather speed then eased the stick further back and she lifted over the trees. Down below me in one corner of the field I saw a great black scar where Matthews had died, then I was passing over the river and climbing with all the power and thrust of the Monosoupape. She laboured a little, but at two thousand feet I did a cautious climbing turn and levelled off. Aeroplanes were still new enough for people to be interested, and all over the town I could see faces upturned and people stopping their cars to get out and watch. They probably thought I was Matthews's successor and was going to treat them to the stunts that barnstormers usually provided to tickle the palates of potential customers and get them out to the field. But this Avro had more to do than merely amuse.

It hadn't been my intention to do much more than fly straight and level, but the old flying bug got hold of me and I let the machine climb, the engine throbbing in a steady rhythm. She flew with the left wing a bit low, but I wasn't worried. Knowing about it, I could correct it.

I banked her and put her into another climb and levelled off at six thousand feet, the big propeller beating. Below, I could see the land as clearly and sharply as in a crystal. To the south nearer to the sea, there was a level plain of cloud, sparkling in the sun, all alabaster castles and snowy valleys, with here and there purple gaps through which I could see the brown of the earth. The light was brilliant and came from every direction at once, as it always does when you are high, and the immense sky was a bowl of brilliant blue, the sun brighter than anyone on earth ever saw it. As high as this, with only the drumming, sighing and creaking of the aeroplane and the smell of oil and exhaust for company, I felt my spirit surge with elation.

This was the way to do it, I thought. We *were* aviators. We *had* to aviate.

The land below was as varied as a mosaic of silks and I sailed along for some time, half-frozen, my face stiff with the cold from the propeller blast. Eventually I became aware how cold I was. My nose was dripping and my feet were numb. I huddled lower out of the blast then, burping the engine to reduce speed, pushed the nose down, circling towards the earth. I picked out the town, then the field and the barn with the group round the Ford truck. A few minutes later I was bumping along the grass and Puddy and Tommy and Red were running towards me, followed by a long string of grinning farm children.

As I switched off and jumped clear, Tommy grabbed my hand and began to pump it.

'She's okay,' he said. 'What happens now?'

'I'm flying straight down to Camarillo,' I said. 'Sling's there, waiting. Bring the DH down as soon as she's fit to fly.'

–

We filled up the tank and I took off again, wearing Mamie Matthews's helmet which Red had provided. She'd worn her hair frizzy in the style of the day and it was too big for me. I couldn't get it tight enough round my chin, so that I had to strain my jaw downwards all the time to hold it firmly on my head and prevent air getting inside and ballooning it.

There was a surging excitement inside me. I was going to war once more! It was only a small war this time, against a bunch of bandits on horses but, whichever way you looked at it, I was going into battle.

Texas to the south-west of San José was dicey country to fly over, and I started to rise at once. I didn't have to fly over the Rocky Mountains, thank God, though they ran all the way down from Canada to Mexico, but, just north of Camarillo, the last few heights petered out in Mount Livermore and Cathedral Mountain, and finally Chinati Peak. I reckoned

I could just get into Camarillo on the petrol I was carrying, and Tommy had found a good map which, even if it wasn't a flying map, at least showed the country well and was on a big scale. For safety I decided to follow the railway line to Marfa, which would bring me to Cathedral Mountain and then I'd have to find Presidio and, just to the west, Camarillo.

I picked up McCamey and Fort Stockton, then I saw the land beneath me begin to rise more steeply. With its ancient Mono engine, the Avro was a lot slower than I'd expected and I studied the compass, tachometer and pressure gauge, the only instruments the machine boasted, and stared anxiously over the blunt snout. The Avro had been the first real aeroplane built in England after the curved wing fragilities that were really only powered box-kites, and this one wasn't much to write home about.

The stink of dope and the bitter nutty tang of castor oil with which the frame and fabric of the old machine were soaked filled my nostrils. I was already growing conscious that this area of the United States wasn't the best flying country in the world and that the old Avro was badly underpowered for flying over it. If, for people like the late Clint Matthews, the world hadn't moved far from the days when a pre-flight check was a twang of the bracing wires, a kick at the tyres and a waggle of the control surfaces, it certainly had for me. After flying through the war – and surviving it – and then in Russia, I'd learned a little about staying alive, and I knew your luck always improved if you took no chances. But what we had to do had to be done fast. The old aeroplane was already worn out, and a little too much Texan sunshine and too many cold nights had played the devil with her.

I looked at my watch and realized I was taking too long, and that Cathedral Mountain was slow coming up. My petrol must be running low by this time, and I began to get the old nervous dry-throated feeling I always got when I began to feel scared.

Then, thank God, I saw the mountain, identified it and turned safely away from it. Now I had to be careful not to fly over the border. Not yet, anyway, or I'd be finding myself having to put her down on the other side through lack of petrol. I was just growing worried again when I caught the sun on the Rio Grande, the river that formed the border, and followed it north-west past Chinati Peak and finally found Camarillo.

It looked pretty small from the air, tucked into a valley near the river with the hills of Texas on one side and the hills of Mexico on the other. It hadn't looked half so small from on the ground, and I suddenly began to wonder if we were mad and if we wouldn't have been wiser to leave it all to Lea-Ferney and the diplomats. But that would probably take weeks. The Foreign Office never moved very fast and at the moment it seemed disinclined to move at all. It was up to us – me, perhaps – and nobody else.

I circled Camarillo, knowing the petrol was low and praying that Slingsby was on the look-out. The sun was pouring down and I could see the land below me, tawny and gold and scarred with age. I could see only one field that looked flat enough to land in, and I hoped that before long somebody would show up, because if something didn't happen soon that was where I was going to have to put her down.

Then I saw a motor car tearing along a yellow road, streaming a long wake of dust behind it. It was heading for the field I'd chosen and I guessed it was Slingsby. Behind it was a string of trucks, buggies and men on horseback, with, behind all that lot, people on foot, running as hard as they could go. Among them was a high-slung black vehicle with glass sides and pompoms at the corner. I guessed it was the hearse; and that Jacob Dibben, the undertaker, was driving it – either coming to see the fun or because he thought he saw business in the offing.

As the car containing Slingsby stopped, I saw him running to the end of the field. From what looked like a pile of dried grass, I saw a puff of smoke which floated away to give me the wind direction, and I swung the Avro over the end of the field and lined up for my final approach. As I turned, I glanced down and saw the field ended in a deep gulch filled with white skeleton-like trees. Then the engine coughed and I knew the petrol was finished and that this was *it.* I either went in or I was going to crash somewhere and fold up the undercart, the propeller and the wings, to say nothing of me.

I was holding her up to stretch out the glide, trying to gauge that nice speed between gliding and stalling, when with a sigh of relief I saw the edge of the field pass back under the wings. Slingsby was there with Evalina and Dan Tucker. Slingsby, like a fool, was flapping a blanket over the fire so that the smoke came out in puffs. I held her off until she settled and finally heard the rumble of the wheels as she touched. Almost at once, I became aware of a madman on a motor-bike tearing along beside me, close enough for him to reach out and touch the wings. It was Young Lukey, and he was waving and grinning all over his face.

I didn't have to switch off the engine. It simply stopped as the tank ran dry. As the machine came to a halt, Slingsby led a mad stampede across the field.

'Sent you a few smoke signals,' he yelled. 'Snake-Eyes showed me how. Real Navajo stuff. Sorry I didn't have time to spell out "Welcome Home" in morse but you probably wouldn't have recognized it, anyway.'

As I jumped down, Evalina flung her arms round me and hugged me. Then she realized the rear cockpit was empty except for ballast.

'Where's Alexei?' she said, and I noticed that she'd dropped the 'Puddy'. 'Where's Tommy?'

I explained what was happening and that they hoped to be down within a day or so. As we talked, the cavalcade from the town arrived, first the hotel proprietor in a car, then the store owner and his family in a truck, taking a day off from sifting through their burnt-out store. Then came the hearse and finally all the buggies and horses and the people on foot. They arrived in the field to stop at a respectful distance before, growing more curious, they began to edge closer to take a look at this phenomenon of a machine that flew. Though, according to Tommy, there'd been Jennies down on the border helping Pershing's punitive expedition, it was clear they hadn't been seen round Camarillo.

As we tried to persuade the kids not to climb all over the wings, explaining that they were pretty fragile and that you could put your feet through them if you weren't careful, Captain O'Hara rode up with half a dozen of his men.

'Thought you might like a guard posted,' he said.

'I certainly would, Captain,' I said. 'Can you persuade the kids not to tear pieces off for souvenirs?'

He grinned and gestured to his men, who handed their reins to a horseholder, hitched at their belts, and went round the Avro, plucking children off as if they were collecting blackberries. After that, it was safe to take your eyes off her for a second.

'There's been another message,' Evalina said. 'It's getting urgent.'

Charley's message was in the same vein as the last – still cheerful, still protesting about the conditions but maintaining that they were safe and that I wasn't to take any risks. She kept up her running commentary of insults about Guzmán, obviously drawing great pleasure from the fact that she thought he couldn't understand.

There was a more ominous note on the back in Guzmán's writing. He was losing patience and would give us no more than four more days to get the rifles he demanded. If they didn't arrive, he proposed to shoot the girls.

The words jarred and I felt cold. I didn't know whether to believe him or not. But there was no answer. There could never be any rifles.

'Does he mean it?' I asked.

Ojarra pulled a face. 'With Guzmán these days, one does not know, *señor*, I think he has become a little *loco*. Otherwise, he would not still be insisting on war when the wars are over. I have seen him treat people with great kindness and then in the next breath pull out his revolver and shoot them down.'

I turned to Slingsby. 'How about petrol?' I asked.

'Ready.' He gestured to the end of the field where I saw cans of petrol stacked up, waiting. 'Enough for a dozen flights, and more where that came from if we need it.'

'Maps?'

'We have 'em. Covering the area for a hundred miles in every direction south of the border.'

'What about the *hacienda*? Can we land there?'

It was Ojarra who answered this time. 'There is a field,' he said. 'This size. No more. But it is half a mile from the *hacienda*. They would see you arrive.'

There were still plenty of problems, it seemed, but Ojarra had thought of that one, too.

'I have a suggestion to make,' he said. 'I will cross the river ahead of you and make for Las Flores. I will be there when you arrive. I shall need forty-eight hours. When you land, I will make a diversion to keep them busy until you have rescued the *señoritas* and escorted them back to the *aeroplano*.' He paused. 'Nevertheless,' he ended, 'it would be a good idea for you to go armed.'

'I'm going armed,' I said grimly. 'And God help friend Esplenderoso if I come face to face with him.'

I glanced at the sky and then at Slingsby. 'Might be a good idea to take a look at the place straight away,' I said. 'Light's good. We ought to be able to see a good distance. That being so, we won't have to go too near and they may not be alarmed. How about doing the old observer act in the rear cockpit?'

Slingsby grinned. 'I'm ready,' he pointed out. I slapped his shoulder. 'Saddle up,' I said.

Chapter 6

I'd done some funny things in my flying career – from shooting down balloons to taking part in a charge of Cossack cavalry, but this was a new one. I was proposing to tackle with an aeroplane a bunch of Mexican bandits on horses who neither respected the law nor had any law to respect.

There still wasn't an official government in Mexico City and there wasn't much order either; and, for once, I wasn't flying a good aeroplane, serviced, tuned and rigged by stolid British fitters and riggers; just an old army cast-off which had been put through God alone knew what stresses by its late last owner. But though she was of patched and dubious quality, I reckoned I had enough skill to make sure she'd carry me and Slingsby over the border and the necessary eighty miles inland.

Half Camarillo had turned up by this time, and it took Captain O'Hara and his men, aided now by the Sheriff and his deputies, who'd turned up in a Ford tourer, to push the crowd back. Mounting his men, Captain O'Hara trotted them up and down in front of the crowd, growing nearer with every turn, until they finally edged back to the fringe of the field. With the area clear, we filled the Avro up, filtering the petrol through a chamois leather that Slingsby had been careful to obtain, because like me, he had no particular wish to come down on the wrong side of the border with a blocked petrol feed.

Neither of us had proper flying clothes, but Captain O'Hara provided a leather campaign over-coat which he loaned to Slingsby who was going to be standing up in the slipstream in the rear cockpit, studying the ground, while Young Lukey dug out an old motoring helmet and a pair of goggles for him. A heavy cavalry coat appeared for me, and O'Hara's sergeant provided a pair of army goggles to make up the complement.

'Look like Richthofen,' Slingsby grinned.

'You ready?'

'*And* willin'. Let's wind up the old clockwork and shove off before we realize what we're goin' to do and back out of it.'

I nodded. Slingsby's nerve was proverbial, but he always made a great show of being frightened to death whenever anything was happening.

We stuffed the maps away carefully and turned the machine down-wind. Ojarra appeared, nervous-looking, near the aeroplane, determined to shake hands as if we were the saviours of his country.

'You will do Mexico a great service,' he said, 'if you could rid her of Guzmán. There will never be peace near the border while he's alive.'

'I'm not going to war,' I pointed out gently. 'I'm just here to do a bit of rescue work. That's all. Don't use me to start a conflict.'

He gave a sad smile. 'I wish I could, *señor*. I shall be ready to hear what you have decided when you return. I now have seven men in the town, with horses and provisions and water. We can leave as soon as you give us the word.'

Captain O'Hara held out a stern soldierly hand. It was like grasping the branch of an oak tree.

'Good luck, son,' he said. 'That is, sir. I gather you outrank me.'

'Not in experience, and certainly not in experience of this place, Captain,' I said.

'I can't go over the border,' he apologized. 'But I'll sure take a chance if you're in trouble. If I hear shooting, I'll be crossing. I guess if I'm saving American lives nobody's going to complain and I can always say I *thought* you were American. You sure got American guts and tenacity.'

'Thanks, Captain. That's a compliment.'

Archie and Snake-Eyes, bow-legged and weathered like old leather, also shook hands, lingering over Slingsby, who seemed somehow with that mad charm of his to have completely captivated them. Dan Tucker gestured. 'Make it good, son,' he said. 'Everything we've got this side of the border's at your disposal.'

'Just keep your fingers crossed for Tommy,' I said. 'We'll pull it off with his help.'

I wasn't so sure we would, but Evalina seemed to think so and she clung happily to me and Slingsby for a second. She was a pretty girl and Slingsby obviously enjoyed it. As we climbed aboard, they all stood back, all of them a little concerned and scared because they knew nothing about aeroplanes.

'Okay?' I shouted to Slingsby.

He nodded and I gestured to Archie. Slingsby had spent half an hour coaching him in propeller-swinging and he approached the machine warily, looking as if he were about to throw a steer.

'He'll probably have it on its back and a brandin' iron on its bum if we're not careful,' Slingsby said.

Archie looked up. 'I'll get chopped in half,' he bleated.

'No, you won't, old lad,' Slingsby said. 'Not if you do as I told you.'

'We-ell – you ready?'

'Ready.'

Archie began to push the propeller round, keeping well back in case the machine started suddenly and made mincemeat of him.

'Contact.'

'Contact.'

I switched on and, spitting on his hands, he grabbed the propeller and leaned back.

As he heaved, there was an immediate roar, and he promptly dived sideways and started running. But the machine was held by the home-made chocks that Lukey had thrown together. Archie recovered quickly and crept forward to grasp one of the ropes. Snake-Eyes grasped the other. Blipping the engine to keep the Avro from overriding them, I decided we'd better go before I frightened them all to death.

As I waved, they hauled the chocks away and we began to taxi down the field in a series of zigzags so I could see my course round the bulbous nose of the machine. At the other end, I swung her straight into wind and let her rip. The tail came up at once as I pushed the stick forward, and she rattled and bumped across the uneven ground.

Ojarra and Captain O'Hara were standing to one side and Dan Tucker had one arm round Evalina, who'd crammed her fists up to her mouth. Archie and Snake-Eyes looked awed, two small bow-legged figures in blue jeans and high-heeled boots and wide, greasy straw hats.

With two people aboard, the Avro took a lot longer to lift her wheels from the ground, and I hoped that the field near the Hacienda Las Flores that Ojarra had mentioned didn't have any obstacles in the way.

The population of Camarillo obviously didn't think we were going to make it; I saw the crowd at the end of the field crumble and start to run, scattering as they made for the dirt road. Then, as we roared over their heads in a climbing turn towards the south, their faces went up and round like a lot of white puddings, turning with us until we'd passed over the edge of the field.

As we lifted over Camarillo, I saw more faces staring up and people in the plaza near the hotel and round the burnt-out store, then a whole lot of handkerchieves started fluttering. If nothing else, we were giving this little wood and *adobe* border town something to talk about.

Slingsby unhitched the Gosport tube in the rear cockpit and started yelling down it.

'River on your right,' he announced. 'Better follow the road. We ought to be able to establish it by findin' the Ford.'

The road into Mexico was a winding dusty red snake. It seemed empty, a thin ribbon like a snail trail between the rocks and the *mesquite.* Almost immediately, we saw it start to climb into the hills, and then damned if we didn't see the Ford, as Slingsby had said. But it was hardly the same Ford. The hood had gone with all the wheels, seats and luggage racks. Clearly the Mexicans had found a use for them and, as we floated over the top of it, I saw a figure in white dart away.

It was only a shell at the side of the road, picked as clean as the carcass of an animal after the vultures had found it. Doubtless at that moment, the Boyce motormeter which had graced the bonnet was acting as an ornament over some Mexican fireplace, probably decorated with feathers and a picture of Our Lady of Guadalupe.

Soon afterwards we passed just to the west of Acizpe. Apart from the church, which was built in Spanish rococo style, it looked not much bigger than a large farm. There seemed to be no sign of life in it and I wondered if the Villistas had left a single living thing there.

'We'll head south, then turn west and come at it from the south,' I suggested. 'They won't be expecting us from that side and when they see us they might imagine we've come from Mexico City way and belong to Obregón. Besides, we'll have the sun behind us from that side and they'll not spot us so easily.'

Using the sun was a dodge as old as air fighting and it was just possible that we could survey our landing strip without being seen.

Swinging southwards, we picked up the railway track towards Chihuahua. It was a long winding snake with the sun shining on the double rails. North of Chihuahua we saw a crowd of horsemen across it and a string of carriages. Then we realized there was no steam coming from the engine and that the carriages looked lopsided, and we guessed that this was where Guzmán had torn up the track and wrecked the train ahead of the one Charley and Dominique Duellin had been travelling on. The men by the track stared up at us as we passed overhead.

Then we saw a long column of horsemen. Their sombreros, catching the sun, made them look like a long caterpillar upside down, with its suckers in the air. They wore every kind of clothing imaginable, from city suits to the white cotton of the *peóns*, and carried the usual array of armament and ammunition. Seeing the weapons, I kept well out of range.

Slingsby pointed to them. 'I'll bet that's some of Villa's lot,' he yelled. 'Headin' for Sabinas. You're seein' somethin', old son, you'll probably never see again.'

The sight of that long straggling column of horsemen moving down a narrow winding *arroyo* which flung the sun back off its tawny sides made me realize how different Mexico was from the rest of the world, even from the United States just across the border. Somehow, I don't know why, they made me think of something left over by the Spanish *Conquistadores* – colourful, dashing but no longer of much value.

Leaving them behind us, we followed the road north to Ciudad Ahumada then swung north-east over the hills. Nothing but a succession of *mesas*, each lifting higher than the last and split up by *arroyos*, it was bad country to fly over and rough to land on, with long dead-end valleys. Pershing's punitive expedition had used Jennies to do their scouting for them but they hadn't helped much; and, though Pershing had brought Villa to account on two or three occasions, they'd mostly been scrambled affairs from which he'd always extricated himself and most of his men.

Finding the road, we watched the scrub bush grow more sparse as it lifted higher, then, quite unexpectedly, as it appeared from behind a clump of trees, we saw the *hacienda*. It was smaller than the Tucker place and consisted of a low white building with a few outhouses and fencing. I saw no animals and I realized it was more or less derelict. Then I saw horses in a small corral to the south.

'Twenty-five of 'em,' Slingsby counted. 'At least! That means twenty-five men. Twenty-three, if the girls had a horse each.'

I opened the throttle and we lifted higher. The afternoon sun was lowering now and the land looked golden-bronze, with long shadows in the *arroyos.* We'd come up from the south and I was still hoping that Splendid Ben and his friends would think we were part of Obregón's army. Obregón was supposed to be near Mexico City in what had been the territory of Villa's twin devil, Emiliano Zapata, until his assassination the previous year, but there were plenty of people on his side operating to the north. Everybody was jumping on his band waggon now and there were plenty of his supporters chasing the late president, Carranza, and more still keeping a sharp eye open in Chihuahua for our old friend, Villa, to appear.

The *hacienda* was at the end of a *mesa* that slipped away in a gentle slope towards a valley. At the front, the valley was shallow and there was a road winding up to the house through the remains of a long shaded drive. The house was built in the form of an L, one arm the residential quarters, the other, longer, arm the out-houses, kitchens and servants' working areas with, at the end, the stables. One part of this longer arm had been destroyed by fire, so that the stable area was separate and only one part at the end still stood, gaunt and ugly beyond the charred remnants, looking like a barn. Beyond the barn, I could see the corral, and beyond that still, a gently sloping pasture that ended with a sheer drop into the valley which curved round from the front of the house, carved deep into the earth at this point and carrying the road north to the border. It was a place that had been built with one eye on the view and the other on defence, and it looked a tough nut to crack. The pasture beyond the corral didn't look very big but it looked big enough to land on – just. Some of the pinched fields we'd used during the war had made us skilled at getting in and out when there wasn't much elbow room.

Slingsby was obviously thinking the same thing. 'We can make it,' he yelled. 'It slopes upwards into wind. That'll make taking off and landing easier.'

'So long as there isn't a gale blowing or the wind isn't across the slope. This damned Mono isn't a very powerful engine. I'm going down to have a look.'

I banked, one eye all the time on the *hacienda*, then, as we came round, dropping all the time, I saw shutters on the south side of the house suddenly flung open and a head appeared. There was a brief wild waving of a handkerchief, then the head was withdrawn and the shutters were closed. Almost immediately, men ran out and started firing at us with rifles and, then, damned if two of them didn't struggle out with what was clearly a machine-gun on a stand.

'By God, they've got a Lewis or somethin',' Slingsby yelled.

'We'd better shove off.'

'I bet they couldn't hit a pig in a passage!'

He was probably right but I didn't intend to find out. I knew all I wanted to. I even knew which room Charley was in, because I knew as certainly as I knew the sun would come up the next morning that the head which had appeared and the handkerchief which had waved had belonged to her. Even if Esplenderoso Benavenides Guzmán did think we came from one of Obregón's supporters, who'd brought the aeroplane from north of the border, I knew damn well that Charley didn't.

She knew her Martin, I was sure. She knew I was sold on flying, and she'd long since given up hope of persuading me to give it up and become a grocer or something. The last time I'd seen her was when I'd set off for Russia months before, but there had never been a let-up in the joyous delight she appeared to get out of writing to me. Her letters always showed her capacity for enjoying life and her complete understanding that, while it might give her a few frights now and again, she could never expect me to give up flying. *She* would know, if nobody else knew, that any aeroplane floating around above the Hacienda Las Flores would be flown by Mark Martin Falconer.

I swung away to the south again, hoping to fool Guzmán that danger was more likely to come from there than from the north. The men with the machine-gun fired a few rounds after us but they came nowhere near us, and I assumed they'd done it as much as anything else for their own conceit and to show Charley and the girl with her what fine fellows they were.

Slingsby was staring back.

'That was a gel,' he yelled. 'In the window!'

'I know,' I yelled back. 'It was Charley.'

'How do you know?'

'I just do, that's all. And I dare bet she knew that this was me.'

Slingsby stared at me through the bug-eyed motoring goggles. 'I reckon you two communicate by telepathy,' he said.

'Not telepathy,' I yelled back. 'It's just knowing. That's all.'

He grinned. 'Bless you, my children,' he said. 'I now declare you man and wife.'

–

We were well south now, eighty miles inside Mexico. Once again, we'd no right to be there, but it had seemed that nobody else was prepared to take the chance. And, just as we swung in a wide arc to turn north again, I saw we weren't alone in the sky.

Slingsby spotted the other aeroplane at the same time and yelled into the Gosport tube. 'It's Tommy!' he said. 'He's got down quicker than he expected and come to find us!'

We grinned at each other, then I took another look at the other plane and noticed that the wings were double strutted and that the top one was much wider than the bottom.

'That's not Tommy,' I yelled. 'That's a Jenny!'

'Perhaps he got hold of a serviceable one and decided to use that instead.'

Whichever way it was, I decided to be wary and headed away from the other machine. It turned after us, however, and as it drew closer I noticed it had three stripes painted on the fuselage in green, white and red, the Mexican colours. Then, as it banked, I saw they were repeated on the upper wing surface.

'That's not Tommy,' I yelled. 'It looks to me like the Mexican Air Force coming to get us for violating their territory! Let's beat it!'

I swung away, trying to edge round the Jenny for the north, but the Jenny had a bigger engine and was faster – and she was across our course.

The sun was like a brass ball in the sky and the clarity in the air was that of a crystal; as the Jenny drew closer, I could see every stitch and patch and turnbuckle – even the oil on the engine cowling. It was manoeuvring to one side, and to my surprise, because I hadn't been expecting it, I saw tracer bullets heading towards us and realized that there was a man in the rear cockpit, and he had a machine-gun and was trying to shoot us down. It seemed to be time to take action.

'Hold tight,' I yelled to Slingsby, and stood the Avro on its wingtip to swing round behind the Jenny. The Jenny, more lumbering despite its bigger engine, followed us round and ended up behind us again. There was no shooting, however, and I decided that it hadn't a gun firing through the propeller, which was something. It seemed to be up to me to keep in front of it.

I didn't know whether it was part of Obregón's army or Carranza's; or even something left over from Huerta or Tómas Urbina, or one of the other villains who'd tried at one time or another in the last ten years to run Mexico; or even whether our friend, Villa, had managed in the end to acquire an aeroplane in spite of us. But certainly somebody had got hold of one and was trying to kill us, and I had to do something about it.

We were heading back towards the high land now, just to the east of the Hacienda Las Flores. Below us I could see the yellow ground split by deep *arroyos* carved into the hills. The Jenny was closing up on us again and if he drew alongside he could shoot us down without us being able to retaliate.

'He's catching up,' Slingsby yelled.

The Jenny was drawing alongside again now and I saw the tracers streaking towards us once more. At first I was angry, then I remembered I had no cause to be. I was violating Mexican territory and, whatever had happened to Charley, I didn't possess that right. But when somebody tries to kill you, the only thing to do is try to kill them back, and I hadn't a gun and couldn't quite see what to do. But then I remembered what Red, Matthews's mechanic, had said while we'd watched Matthews preparing to kill himself.

'Any mountain over five thousand feet's too high to climb over,' he'd said. 'So you gotta go between 'em down the canyons. And, brother, you sure gotta be careful the one you choose don't come to a dead end.'

It seemed I had a weapon after all, even if it were only experience. I pushed the nose down and dropped close to the earth. The ground looked bleak and horrifyingly dangerous. The Jenny pilot didn't seem to like being quite so close to the earth and dropped back a little to think it out. Then he opened the throttle and came after me, crowding up behind, and I guessed that, since he couldn't use the rear-firing gun, he was going to try to force us into the ground.

But two could play at that game and I spotted a wide canyon and dived into it. The Jenny came after me, forced to stay behind us because of its narrowness. For a mile or two the canyon turned right and then left and we flew along it, the walls terrifyingly close – so close you could pick out individual rocks and caves.

I glanced back to see where the Jenny was and caught a glimpse of Slingsby's face. He looked petrified. I didn't blame him. I was, too, because the valley was growing narrower.

The Jenny was crowding up on our tail now and I could see the pilot's head. I knew he wouldn't dare chew up our rudder with his propeller, though, because it would be the end of him, too, in the sort of territory we were flying over. He was probably some renegade American or Englishman, or perhaps an ex-German Air Service flier who could no longer find employment in his own country since the war. But he could certainly fly and he followed me down the narrow valley expertly, knowing that as soon as we were clear of it he could draw alongside again for his observer to fill us full of bullets.

But he was so concerned with keeping close to us, he probably hadn't noticed what I'd spotted from above. The valley came to a dead end a few miles further on. He was a little lower than we were now, just behind our tail, his eyes fixed on us so that he couldn't have seen the blank red wall of earth and stone which was coming up. I held on as long as I dared, terrifying myself as well as Slingsby, then, at the last moment, hauled back on the stick.

The Avro, bless her, behaved like all Avros, with the docility of a well-trained horse. She lifted at once, soaring up, the Mono screaming and sending the echoes hammering along the canyon walls. Her wheels just scraped the edge of the dead end of the canyon, and then we were clear and into honest-to-god clear air with room to manoeuvre. The Jenny pilot was just a little later reacting and he'd been lower to start off with, and as we soared over the flat plain beyond the canyon, I glanced back and saw at once that he'd left it too late and wasn't going to make it. Despite his bigger engine, the machine was labouring and the wheels caught the edge of the canyon wall in a puff of dust and a cloud of flying stones. The machine's nose dipped and dug into the earth, and I saw a piece of the propeller fly into the air, then the Jenny was slithering along through the dust, breaking up as it went. A wing fell off and then another, then the fuselage slewed round and slithered sideways for a while. Then the engine fell out of its mountings, and the fuselage broke in two and the whole thing came to a stop in a huge rising cloud of dust.

Slingsby was pounding my shoulder as we circled the wreckage, staring down. Below, I saw a man appear from the cloud of dust, and then another. I was glad they'd survived. It was a spectacular crash, but wood-and-canvas machines gave a crew a chance and I was glad I hadn't killed them. I had no quarrel with them and they'd been in the right defending their territory, whoever they were.

We were still circling when I spotted a troop of horsemen galloping towards the aeroplane, dragging a cart that seemed to be mounted with a Vickers machine-gun. They didn't look like Villa's men in ragged clothes and sombreros, but wore some semblance of uniform and bus conductor's hats. I had no idea who they were but they seemed to be official and as we passed over them, they let loose a volley of shots from the saddle.

'Time we were on our way,' Slingsby yelled.

Camarillo seemed to have given us up. As we crossed the river back into the States, there was a string of vehicles heading back into town from the field, led by the proprietor of the hotel in his black Ford. But, as soon as they saw us, they stopped and I saw them backing and filling as they turned their cars in the road and hauled their horses round to set off back to the field.

The hearse hadn't moved. Quite clearly, Dibben the undertaker still had hopes we'd provide him with business. Anybody heading for revolutionary Mexico was always potential business for him, I expect; and in an aeroplane I suppose doubly so. I imagine he was hoping somebody had shot at least one of us.

Evalina was jumping up and down with delight as we swung over the end of the field into wind and came down.

The crowd had lined the field and I could see them waving handkerchieves and the Stars and Stripes, even the old Stars and Bars, the flag of the Southern states in the Civil War. They were obviously glad to see us waving back – except perhaps Dibben – then, just as we were coming in, some damn fool of a kid at the reins of a buggy decided he'd get a better view from the other side of the field, and pulled out from the crowd. Whipping up the two mules, he set off at a gallop right across our flight path.

I'd almost touched down when I first saw him out of the corner of my eye, and I could just imagine the wind-milling propeller mincing him up. Opening the throttle, I hauled on the stick and we lifted again. But we hadn't got flying speed because we were almost down and we just scraped above the buggy as it passed across the nose. The boy had flung himself off, his eyes wide with terror as he saw himself being carved up by the whirling brass ends of the propeller, but the cart went clattering on right across our path. I felt a crunch below me as we passed over the bucketing vehicle and, out of the corner of my eye, saw a piece of wood flying through the air. But we were still flying and I decided we'd made it, and was more concerned for a moment with Slingsby who was hanging so far out of the machine to shake his fist at the terrified boy, I thought he'd fall out.

As we came round again, though, I saw Captain O'Hara staring up at us with a pair of binoculars to his eyes, then he dropped them on his chest and started to gallop down the field, waving his arms. For a moment I wondered what the devil he was up to, then I saw Lukey Morro's motor-bike roar out from the crowd and start turning in narrow circles in the middle of the landing strip, Young Lukey waving and pointing at his front wheel. As it dawned on me what he was trying to tell me, I looked over the edge of the cockpit and, staring down, saw the starboard undercarriage wheel twisted wildly out of shape on a bent axle-end.

Chapter 7

My heart sank. This was going to finish us – just when we'd found out for certain where Charley was – because we wouldn't be able to pick up yet another aeroplane as easily as we'd picked up this one.

Captain O'Hara had swung round in the middle of the field now and was chasing the terrified buggy-driver back to the crowd. A man grabbed him and I saw him walloping him as hard as he could, then the boy broke loose and bolted for Camarillo, and I guessed there'd be a few harsh words round the town that night. One of O'Hara's troopers had caught up with the fleeing buggy and, leaning from the saddle, had grasped the bridle of one of the mules and hauled it to a stop at the far side of the field.

For a while I flew round, wondering what to do. If I could get the Avro down in one piece we might just salvage the operation: the wingtips had skids on them that might protect them, and aeroplanes were always stronger than they looked. We might scrape a bit of fabric off but that could always be repaired quickly, even if I had to go on my knees to Camarillo housewives for their Sunday-best Irish linen tablecloths. At that moment, now that I'd found Charley, I'd not even have said no to a bit of bed ticking.

Slingsby was peering over the side, trying to get a look at the wheel. It was harder from the rear cockpit and once again I thought he might fall out. My mind was racing. The one thing I had to do was preserve the propeller. There probably wasn't another Avro airscrew before you got to Houston and probably not even there. The Avro was a British aeroplane and they were few and far between in the States, unlike SE5s and De Havillands which had been built there under licence during the war.

'What are we goin' to do?' Slingsby yelled.

'Well, we can't stay up here for ever,' I said. 'I'll try to get in on one wheel.'

'Think you can do it?'

'Your guess is as good as mine.'

We came round over the end of the field again and I could see every face turned up to us. Evalina had stopped jumping up and down, and had her clenched fists to her mouth once more.

'Hold your hat on,' I said. 'Here we go.'

I side-slipped into position to take off some of the speed and we slipped over the edge of the field, starboard wing high in the air. It was going to be a tricky job because if I got the port wing too low, that one would touch instead. I had to gauge it exactly and I'd got to let her roll to a stop as slowly as possible before I let the starboard wing go down. The difference between doing damage and making it safely was pretty fine.

I flipped up the main switch. The engine milled round for a while then stopped, and I switched off the petrol and shuffled a little in my seat to make myself comfortable.

'Hang on.'

Slingsby crouched down in the rear cockpit. If we stood on our nose, he'd probably shoot out over the wing and land on his head. I'd seen more than one observer break his neck that way. But he waved cheerfully as we floated down and braced himself with elbows, hands and knees as we came over the edge of the field. I held her off as long as I could until she was only just drifting in. The green of the field changed to individual blades of grass but she was still floating in with the starboard wing in the air. Then I heard the port wheel rumble as it touched the ground, stop, and rumble again. This time the rumble continued and the plane rattled as it rolled over the uneven ground while I held the starboard wing up, letting the plane find its own time to settle. She rolled on just a little further then, as the speed dropped, the starboard wing sagged slowly down. The bent wheel turned, jammed, screeched in protest, and collapsed, then the wing touched the ground with its skid and wrenched the machine round in a gentle ground loop and we came to a stop. The nose was still up in the air and the propeller was undamaged.

Slingsby let out a yell of relief. 'If you weren't so damn clever with an aeroplane,' he said, 'I'd suggest you were the luckiest beggar alive.'

'No trouble,' I said shakily. 'Every time a coconut.'

But I knew as well as he did how fortunate we'd been.

As we climbed down, the Sheriff's car roared up. I thought the old idiot was going to hit the wing and undo all the good we'd done, but he slammed on the brakes at the last minute and skidded to a stop with locked wheels.

'I got the kid,' he said. 'I got him under arrest.'

I sighed, feeling extraordinarily tired. It had been a long day. 'Let him go,' I said. 'He won't do it again.'

'You sure, Major?'

'Sure I'm sure. Let him go. I reckon the poor kid'll go through it enough from his pals.'

I climbed out and stared at the smashed wheel and bent axle, sick with dismay. After taking on what was probably the whole of the Mexican Air Force and, with a bit of luck, destroying it, we had to suffer this.

Despite what I'd said, if I could have laid my hands on the boy at that moment, I'd probably have beaten the living daylights out of him. With so much depending on precision and time, the shattered wheel could set us all back a couple of days.

Slingsby's eyes were narrow. 'Where in God's name do we get a spare?' he asked.

An idea occurred to me. I remembered Young Lukey on his Moto-Rêve, square-tanked, green-and-grey-painted, its narrow wheels just about the size of an aeroplane wheel.

'Motor-bikes,' I said.

'What's that?'

'Motor-bikes. Young Lukey's got a motor-bike. He'll probably let us have his front wheel.'

'Suppose it's the wrong size?'

'Perhaps he's got a spare. That'll make two. We can get him to turn us a new axle. Good God, we can jack this thing up in no time. It isn't heavy.'

'Will it work?'

'Trouble with you,' I said, 'you haven't been flying very long. In 1914 and 1915, Blériot tails were bolted on Avro fuselages, and undercarts designed for Moranes were bent a bit and fixed to BE8s. Engines intended for Farmans were stuffed into RE2s and so on – and they all seemed to fly. I reckon we ought to be able to fly this thing off with a couple of motor-bike wheels.'

By this time the crowd was sprinting up the field, led by Dan Tucker in the Franklin, with Evalina and an awed Snake-Eyes in the back. Archie MacTaggart was clinging to the running board. Evalina was out of the car before it stopped and running towards us, the divided leather skirt flapping. Flinging her arms round me, she kissed me wildly. She seemed to like flinging her arms round aviators and kissing them; perhaps she was getting into practice for Puddy.

'Thank God,' she said. 'I thought you'd be certain to crash.'

'Evalina, my love,' Slingsby said. 'We damn near did. But for the brilliance and skill of our small dark-haired friend here with the broken nose, I think we would have done. As it is, we're down with a minimum of damage, all of which can be repaired.' He cleared his throat. 'And while we're at it, if you've any spare hugs and kisses goin', I wouldn't ever say no.'

She giggled and repeated her performance for him.

'I'll tell you something else now,' he said. 'We just destroyed the Mexican Air Force.'

'You did what?'

Slingsby repeated the words and there were looks of bewilderment. He explained what had happened and everybody started to grin.

'Without a gun?'

'Without a gun. Thanks once more to our small dark-haired friend.'

The aeroplane was surrounded by people now and still more cars and buggies kept rattling up.

'We ought to do like Clint Matthews and charge an entrance fee,' Slingsby suggested. 'We could make a fortune.'

More cars arrived, then round the back of the crowd I heard the wonderful full-throated snarl of Young Lukey Morro's Moto-Rêve, and he came howling round the tail of the Avro to pull up and sit astride the machine, grinning.

'Kinda bent,' he said.

'Grab him, Sling,' I said.

Slingsby nodded to the Sheriff and I saw them march up to Lukey. He began to protest and the Sheriff put a heavy hand on his shoulder and started heaving. Unwillingly, he allowed himself to be dragged forward, wheeling the motor-bike. Standing alongside me, he blushed and gave his sheepish grin.

I pointed at the motor-bike. 'I want your front wheel, Lukey,' I said.

'Gee, no!' The Moto-Rêve was Lukey's pride and joy. 'I built me a motor-bike here, and I aim to keep it.'

'I don't want your blasted bike,' I said – sharply, because I was tired and I was worried and I could still see that picture of Charley's head appearing and the waving handkerchief. 'I just want the wheel. I want it for the aeroplane.'

He gaped. 'It's a different size. You'd run all cock-eyed with one wheel bigger than the other.'

'I just put her down with no wheel at all on one side,' I said. 'What about that? You can have it back afterwards. In fact, if we pull it off, I'll buy you a *new* bike. I reckon I can afford it – just.'

He looked bashful. 'Aw, no,' he said. 'Y'all don't have to do that. I'll lend you the wheel with pleasure if it's gonna help git that pore young girl outa the hands of them ruffians.'

I could have collapsed with relief. Thank the Lord for the everlasting generosity of Americans, I thought.

'All the same—' Lukey gestured, '—I got a better idea. I got a coupla wheels back at my place. In fact, I got five. Two off an Indian, and three off a BSA and side car. How about using the front wheel of the BSA and the side-car wheel? They're the same size and they ain't got no driving cogs on 'em. I guess I could turn you an axle for 'em long enough to go through them there holes on your aeroplane.'

I grinned at him. 'Lukey,' I said. 'You're the original good Samaritan.'

He shuffled his feet. 'Naw, I ain't no Samaritan,' he said. 'I just don't wanna give up my old bike.'

–

The whole town joined in the job. By this time, they'd heard of the fight with the Mexican aeroplane and they were thoroughly enjoying it, feeling somebody had got their own back for them after the raid. There was only a bit of scraped linen on the wingtip and a tear on the underside, but the ribs and strengtheners were undamaged, and we had the offer of linen and dope and glue within minutes. Dibben, the undertaker, seeing there was no business for him, shot off to town and was back within half an hour with planks and the settles on which he rested the coffins in his undertaking emporium, and with them we lifted the aeroplane off its wheels. We didn't need cranes or lifts because we had the whole population of Camarillo to help. They were all as involved in the rescue operation by this time as we were, and together, balancing the aeroplane on one wheel, we rolled her up a plank until the starboard wing was off the ground, then, holding her horizontal, we used Dibben's settles and planks at the wing roots to hold her up, straight and level so we could take off the wheels and strip the axle clear. As we struggled, I noticed for the first time that Slingsby had the maddening habit of whistling through his teeth all the time as he worked.

With a boy on his pillion holding the bent axle, Lukey roared off on the Moto-Rêve towards his garage to start work at once, while the rest of us occupied ourselves in tying the machine down for the night. I had no wish for one of the Texas whirlwinds to lift her off her settles and drop her down on her wheel-less undercart.

The night was quiet, however, a silent night full of stars, but from the hotel where we ate a meal we were desperately in need of by this time, I could hear Lukey's lathe going down the street.

Someone was playing a guitar in the shadows. '*Adelita*,' Evalina pointed out. 'One of the revolutionary songs from over the border. It's about a girl. It must be one of the Mexican helpers.'

The tune changed to *La Cucaracha*, then went into the more haunting *La Paloma*. The moon seemed like a huge silver ball hanging in the sky and there were all the night scents of flowers and dry earth and trees all round me, and I decided just then that, if it weren't for Charley and what we were contemplating, I wouldn't have minded staying in Camarillo for the rest of my life.

–

We didn't have to ask Lukey to work all night. He did it without a word from us.

We were up with the first light next morning, but he was already there, outside the hotel with the axle and two motor-bike wheels.

'That there,' he said, pointing, 'should just about do the trick.'

Slingsby grinned. 'Lukey,' he said. 'If you were prettier, I'd kiss you.'

Lukey gave a guffaw of laughter. 'Gee, I sure hope not,' he said.

The father of the boy who'd wrecked the Avro was waiting to apologize, so we persuaded him to put the wheels in the back of his buggy, and drove out to the field with Lukey following on his motor-bike. We had the wheels back in place by breakfast-time and, with help from O'Hara's cavalrymen and Lukey and the farmer, had the old aeroplane on the ground again in no time. She seemed to sigh as she settled on her shock absorbers.

'Like an old man getting his crutches back,' Slingsby observed.

I was getting edgy and irritable again. I'd spent most of the night unable to sleep, with that picture of Charley's head appearing at the window and her arm waving frantically. I was still certain it was Charley and I knew she'd known it was me giving the place the once-over with an aeroplane. To Charley it would be the most natural thing in the world to assume I'd do a recce from the air.

We were tucking into one of those enormous American breakfasts of ham, potatoes, hominy, biscuits and coffee, and even the Mexican waitress who served us seemed to be trying to show sympathy and enthusiasm at the same time. As we were finishing the coffee, the landlord brought in an El Paso newspaper which had just come in by car from the railway at Marfa. Carranza had been caught at last by Obregón's supporters and shot dead in some squalid village called San Antonio Tlaxcalantongo, trapped in a primitive hut of wood and thatch. Good red-blooded American reporting gave all the gory details. As he slept under a single blanket with his saddle for a pillow, his enemies had burst into the hut and riddled him with bullets before stealing all his belongings, including even his spectacles. It was as grim and sordid a murder as had come out of the whole revolution, but at least it seemed to have put paid to the troubles. With Villa wanting to retire, it seemed there was no one now to oppose the new candidate, Obregón – and that, at least, was a change.

The newspaper had also got hold of the news of Charley and Dominique Duellin and didn't seem to know which to make the big story, 'GIRLS KIDNAPED,' it screamed in good transatlantic spelling. 'GUZMÁN RAIDS CAMARILLO.'

'They've got it all here, Brat,' Slingsby said, reading aloud. 'Even you – Major Martin Falconer, British wartime ace.'

'I expect somebody here telephoned the story.'

'Anxious to help, shouldn't wonder.'

'I wish they hadn't.'

'Why not?'

'So far, only the people in Camarillo and one or two in San José knew about us. Now half America will get on to it and there'll be a bunch of reporters down here in no time. And you know what big-time American reporters are like.' I gestured. 'You've only got to look at that paper.'

'They *are* a bit over-enthusiastic,' he admitted. 'But what's the harm?'

'If it gets out what we're up to, what's to stop some sympathetic *muchacho* who's come across the river to work here taking the information back with him at night and passing it on to Guzmán. That could sink us.'

Slingsby's jaw fell. 'I suppose you're right.'

By the time Dan Tucker and Evalina appeared for breakfast, a cable had arrived from Tommy.

'*DH going well. With you in twenty-four hours.*'

It seemed twenty hours too long to me. I had a suspicion that things were beginning to drag out too much, and my suspicions were confirmed later in the morning when the old man on the mule appeared from across the river. He had another note from Guzmán and this time, ominously, it wasn't accompanied by anything from Charley. Ojarra translated it for us.

'I am growing impatient,' Guzmán announced. 'Because of this, I have decided to ask also for twenty thousand dollars.'

'He's got the wind up,' O'Hara said. 'He'll have heard about Carranza. The revolution's just about come to an end and, now that Carranza's gone, Obregón'll be able to concern himself with any pockets of resistance that still exist like Guzmán. He obviously wants to get out of the country, but he obviously hasn't the dough to do it with. Four hundred rifles, with the twenty thousand bucks he's asked for, would see him to his old age in comfort in Brazil or Argentina.'

'We need another forty-eight hours,' I said.

O'Hara frowned. 'If sump'n doesn't happen soon, Major, that guy's going to get the breeze-up and probably kill those girls and bolt.'

'We've got to keep him waiting.'

'I guess mebbe he won't want to wait.'

'Is he greedy?' I asked Ojarra.

'*Quién sabe?* I think he is now. He likes fine clothes and good horses, and he needs money to escape.'

'Well, let's tell him we're having difficulty getting the rifles together but that we think we can raise the money more quickly if he'll give us just another couple of days. Tell him we're prepared to pay for the lives of the girls, but we'll have to make arrangements with the bank.'

O'Hara frowned. 'Are we prepared?'

Dan Tucker's mouth was like a rat-trap. 'Sure are,' he said. 'But only if everything else fails. Americans don't like being pushed around. And Guzmán's as treacherous as a rattlesnake.'

'I guess we can get a note to him then,' O'Hara said.

'Why not tell him we'll pay him in silver dollars?' Evalina said. 'Mexicans like coinage better than paper money.'

'Might work,' O'Hara agreed. 'Okay, we'll send him a message.'

He gestured at the old deaf-mute and they vanished towards the saddlery where he and his troop had made their headquarters. I stared at the sky to the north. My fingers were crossed and I was quietly praying that nothing would go wrong with the DH. *We* were ready. Now it all depended on Tommy.

–

I don't think I've lived through a longer day. I spent half the time with my eyes on the sky and the line of blue mountains to the north, hoping all the time to see the DH appearing early, a tiny dot in the sky.

But the sky remained empty, blue and brassy in the sunshine. The town was somnolent in the heat. A few people kept their eyes on the hotel, but nothing was happening and only a few like Lukey and O'Hara were in the know. We said little to Sheriff because we didn't trust him. He seemed to spend every evening in his office with a bottle of *tequila* from across the border on his desk. I thought he was slow and inefficient and not very clever, and preferred to deal with Dan Tucker and Captain O'Hara.

During the morning I took the Avro up. The wheels worked perfectly. They were noisier as she trundled about the field because Lukey's axle wasn't such a good fit as the original but it was quite adequate. The Mono was working well, its full-throated crackling roar reassuring, but all the same we checked all oil and fuel feed lines because we wanted no trouble. Not being expert mechanics, we also called in Lukey to look at the engine, but he wasn't an aero engine expert either and he could only check the same sort of things we'd checked. We stared solemnly at the engine from every angle and had to accept that we had to just hope for good luck and perhaps a helping hand from the Almighty.

We had a last conference with Ojarra after lunch. We'd worked out what we were going to do and we needed him near the Hacienda Las Flores for when we arrived. He promised to light a fire to give us the wind direction and to let us know he was in position. It was going to be his job to keep Guzmán busy while we came at him from the other side. If we failed, he was to try to pull it off on his own and rescue the lot of us by horseback, but we didn't fancy that because Ojarra could produce only seven reliable men and we had an idea by this time that Guzmán had more than the two dozen we'd counted, who'd all be behind walls while we'd be out in the open.

Ojarra promised to provide spare horses, in case, for some reason, we couldn't get the aeroplanes off again, but I hoped we wouldn't need them because it was a long ride to the border from the *hacienda* and we'd heard that Guzmán had friends in the area, too. Ojarra also drew a plan of the *hacienda*. He'd visited it often in its heyday before the revolution when its owner was still alive. After his death in 1913, the family had disappeared on the long march from Chihuahua City when Villa had turned out the hated *gachupíns* and sent them across the Bolsón de Mapiní, a vast sunken depression of baked mud and blistering sand towards Torreón, forbidding them the railway, so that out of five thousand people an appalling number had died. He was able to draw the place from memory, showing the long rooms, the stables, the barns, and what was left of the *hacienda* with its long halls and cool corridors and the smaller rooms which had been the offices of *mayordomos* or butlers. From it we were able to pick out exactly where Charley and Dominique Duellin were kept. It had once been the *mayordomo*'s sitting-room and was on the side from which we'd be approaching.

'But it will be shuttered, *señor*,' Ojarra pointed out. 'It will be impossible to get in through the window. They will never allow them to be opened from outside because by that time, my men will be firing at the house and they will use it as a fortress. You will have to use the door at the back, opposite the barn. Perhaps that will not be so well guarded.'

'Is it heavy?'

'Not as heavy as the front because it was meant less for show. In fact, I think it has been smashed down and a mere plank door put in its place.'

'Suppose it's locked?'

'Then you will have to kick it in, *señor*.'

'Pity we haven't Krupp on our side in this affair,' Slingsby said. 'A few heavy cannon might have helped.'

As Ojarra and his men cantered off, Slingsby and I got down to the plan again. It seemed sound enough but an awful lot seemed to depend on Ojarra. You had to face it, aeroplanes were fine for attacking anything, provided they had guns. And we hadn't. And you couldn't capture buildings with them. In the end, we decided that the best thing to do would be to let Puddy and Tommy, who were the biggest of the four of us – Puddy was tall and Tommy was Texan colossal – pilot the two machines, while Slingsby and I constituted what Slingsby insisted on calling the Camarillo Aerial Striking Force. After landing, while – we hoped – Ojarra was keeping Guzmán and his men busy, we'd leave the aeroplanes and head for the *rancho*, rescue the girls and bolt back while Ojarra helped by picking off anybody who tried to follow. We'd then cram one of us and one of the girls into each rear cockpit and leave the flying to Tommy and Puddy. It sounded fine because neither Slingsby nor

I were heavyweights and we thought we could do it. It would be chancy and an uncomfortable trip, but it wouldn't last for much more than an hour.

'Might even enjoy it,' Slingsby observed. 'Jammed up close like that to a pretty gel, eh?' He paused. 'I can take it this Dominique Duellin is pretty?'

We went over the plan again and again. It wasn't all that hot when we thought of it in cold blood, but it was the only one that would work – if we managed to get off again three up; if Guzmán didn't stop us landing and reaching the *rancho* in the first place; and if the ancient aeroplanes didn't let us down at the last minute.

'When you think about it,' Slingsby said, 'there are a lot of "ifs" in this thing.'

'If you can think of a better idea,' I said, 'I'd be pleased to hear it.'

He sighed. 'Pity O'Hara can't lay on another punitive expedition.'

'They'd see him coming a mile off and bolt,' I pointed out. 'The only way we can get within reach of him in time to stop him bolting is with aeroplanes.'

'He'll still see us comin'.'

'Only a few minutes before we arrive. By that time, he won't have the chance to go far and Ojarra might get the chance to catch him napping.' I stopped. 'Especially if we do it the old way,' I ended.

Slingsby frowned. 'What old way?'

'Dawn patrol. Take off at first light. We'd be putting down before they're awake. Besides, for all we know, there might be another Jenny waiting for us – or even something more lethal. If we go in early it might not be around.'

'Why not take off in the dark?' Slingsby suggested, enthusiastic at once. 'We've all done it at one time or another.'

'The field here's pretty small for that,' I pointed out.

'Why not have a flare path?'

'How?'

'Motor cars. There are a few in this place. They could shine their headlights down the field and even give us a limit marker. And there are plenty of oil lamps and torches. It'd be enough for us to get off. That way, we'd arrive over the border before dawn and we could be puttin' down at Las Flores at first light. I'll bet those lazy blighters won't have a sentry, and we could be among 'em before you could say Giovanni Robinson, or whatever it is the Mexicans say.'

'Don't kid yourself,' I said. 'With the Avro, they'd hear us a mile off.'

'Right. Why not come in with the engine switched off?'

'Suppose it wouldn't start again?'

'We can check and re-check her to make sure she's in good trim. Then as soon as we've landed, one of us could swing the prop to start her again and we can leave the rest to Puddy or Tommy, whoever has her.'

I smiled. 'It might work,' I said. 'Let's go and see O'Hara.'

–

It was quite clear that one of Guzmán's people wasn't far away on the other side of the river, because that evening O'Hara's message was answered by another, brought once more by the old deaf-mute on the mule. Guzmán was obviously growing worried because, though he gave us forty-eight hours to deliver the goods, he made it clear there would be no more extensions after that. We decided it was enough, but only just enough, and I found myself praying once more that nothing would happen to Tommy. We were expecting him the following morning, and the morning after we'd have to do the rescue.

'I wish we'd got a Vickers or two,' Slingsby said, and I found he was echoing my own thoughts. As far as I was concerned we were at war. Perhaps not on the scale we'd seen it in France and Russia, but it was war all the same, against a small group of insurgents holding not only two girls but a whole way of life to ransom, and a machine-gun would have helped.

'We could have chased 'em out somehow,' Slingsby went on wistfully, 'and then caught 'em in the open. Splendid Ben wouldn't kidnap anybody else for a bit if we did.'

'If I come face to face with him,' I growled, 'he won't, anyway. I'm not going unarmed, don't you fret.'

Slingsby gave me a small smile. 'Oddly enough,' he said, 'I wasn't doin'.' He paused. 'What if it doesn't come off?'

'It's got to.'

'Brat, it might not. Suppose, for example, we manage to reach the girls and get 'em out. But suppose we can't get back to the aeroplanes and they have to leave without us.'

'Then we've got to arrange for them to come back and pick us up later.'

'How would they know we were there?'

'We'll arrange a signal. Light a fire. Flash them with a mirror or something. For safety, perhaps we'd better do both, then Splendid Ben won't be able to kid them into landing when we're not there. Got a pocket mirror?'

Slingsby grinned. 'I've noticed Evalina shoving powder on her nose,' he said. 'I'll bet she's got one.'

'I'll get another one from somewhere, and I'll bet Charley hasn't exactly neglected her appearance. She'll have contrived to get one from Splendid Ben, I'll bet, so we'll bring it away with us because it'll doubtless be bigger and work better. We might even borrow a Very pistol from O'Hara if he's got one.'

We discussed the plan we'd made again, thinking of it from every angle before deciding there was little else we could do beyond getting Captain O'Hara to charge with his troop over the border with Dan Tucker and a posse of his cowhands. Either way, there was going to be a lot to answer for from the United States government and O'Hara was in Camarillo to stop that very thing.

The day seemed endless and I was glad when the sun began to slip behind the mountains. We'd just returned to the hotel with Tucker and Evalina for a meal when Lukey's little brother who carried cables for the Post Office arrived. O'Hara was sitting at the next table and beyond him the Sheriff, fat and comfortable, with a bottle on which it said 'Mouthwash' but which I knew was good Mexican *tequila*.

Lukey's brother came across the dining-room and handed over a whole handful of buff forms.

'All for me?' I said.

'Sure are, Major, sir.'

'Seems we've stirred something up.'

'Sure have, Major, sir.'

I looked up. 'You've read 'em?'

'Always do, Major, sir.' He grinned. 'Only bit of fun there is in this dorp, apart from watching the hotel lights go on when the sun sets.'

He even seemed to have put them in the right order of mounting importance. The first one was from Tommy and it lifted our hearts. '*With you first thing tomorrow*,' he'd cabled. No more, but it was enough. We'd be awake at first light with a fire ready at the end of the field to welcome them in.

I passed the form across to Dan Tucker and Evalina. The old man grunted, as though he expected that a Tucker, and a Texan, could do no less. Evalina gave a grin of delight and squeezed my hand.

There were three other cables, two of them from Ludo Sykes, who'd been my commanding officer when we'd left Novorissiisk – how long ago now? Weeks? Months? Years? It was addressed to me and Slingsby. I noticed he'd left off Puddy, who was officially a Russian officer, anyway, and Tommy, who, I suspect, he didn't expect ever to get back to Europe. '*Unofficial leave not – repeat not – permitted. Sykes. Col.*' It seemed to have been originated at Gibraltar and routed via Washington, Houston and San José. I passed it across to Slingsby without comment. The second cable had been sent a day later and it said, '*Heard about Charley. Leave permitted. Good luck. Ludo.*'

I pushed that one at Slingsby, too. At least somebody in the world was human, and of course it had to be Ludo Sykes, Charley's cousin, whom I'd hero-worshipped ever since I'd first met him. Doubtless, he'd got all the Bartelott-Dyveton-Sykeses in Whitehall, at the War Office, the Air Ministry and the Admiralty – and despite the casualties the family had suffered during the recent war, there were still a few – rallying round, pulling strings and threatening Prime Ministers. It gave me a comfortable feeling that what we were intending was approved somewhere. Not much point in being involved with a great family, I decided, if you couldn't get something out of it.

Slingsby grinned but I could see he was relieved, all the same. We'd already spent far longer in the States than we'd originally intended and there'd be quite a lot of questions asked when we got back to the fold. The last of the telegrams was, surprisingly, from Lea-Ferney. '*Clawing at a few throats in Washington,*' it said. '*Have obtained permission for cavalry troop to back you up. Not – repeat not – more than five miles beyond border.*'

It wasn't much but it was something. If it came to a dash for home, O'Hara would be there to help and I hadn't the slightest doubt he'd manage to stretch five miles to ten and even twenty at a pinch. It was nice to think that, if it came to a running fight, he'd be there to help Ojarra.

I passed the telegram across to the Captain at the next table. He fished in his pocket and dragged out a battered spectacle-case. From that he dug out a pair of steel army-issue spectacles which had been broken and repaired with black insulating tape. They made him look like an owl but, as he read, his honest Irish face lit up and dissolved into a mass of leathery creases. I'd never seen him smile before, because he'd always been rather solemn and dignified with us up to then, and it came as a surprise because it quite transformed his grim military face.

'I'm sure pleased to be able to help, Major,' he announced in formal tones. 'I'll be there, don't worry – saddled up, ammunitioned, fed, watered and provisioned. Just give me a chance at that Guzmán guy and he'll wonder what hit him.'

It was an encouraging reaction, and Slingsby grinned. 'Somebody must have been quick on the ball,' he observed, 'to have got the news across the Atlantic.'

'Some bright boy from San José,' I suggested.

'El Paso actually,' a voice said, and we turned round to see a man in a bow tie and straw hat standing by the table. 'Hugh Tweedie Moat,' he announced. '*El Paso Examiner*. That news came up the line from

Marfa and, when I'd checked it, I passed it on to Houston and the news agencies. I guess *they* passed it on to Europe. I stand to make a buck or two outa that. Would you object if I sat down?'

'Go ahead,' I said.

He sat down, took out a cigarette pack and held it up. 'How about the old coffin nail? Mind if I smoke?'

'You can burst into flames if you like,' I said. I had a feeling I wasn't going to like Hugh Tweedie Moat. So far we'd had nothing but sympathy and help, but this one was different. He had hard eyes and a polished sort of face, as if he knew all the answers and wasn't too bothered about people's feelings.

He lit a cigarette and blew out smoke. 'You'll be Major Falconer, I guess,' he went on. 'Major Mark Martin Falconer, Distinguished Service Order, Military Cross, French Legion of—'

'Yes,' I said hurriedly as I saw O'Hara's eyebrows shoot up almost out of sight under his hairline. 'That's right.'

Moat eyed me for a while. 'You're a whole lot younger than I expected, Major,' he said.

Slingsby sniffed. 'He was born rather late,' he said. 'With wings and ailerons already attached. He's really a bird, you know. You should see him fly.'

The man in the bow tie looked surprised, then his expression changed to a smile. 'I heard about that there landing of yours out at old Lukey Morro's field,' he said. 'One wheel. Wow! They tell me you met Villa.'

'Yes.'

'What's he like?'

'Two legs,' Slingsby said. 'Two arms. Both with hands on the ends. Head with real eyes, and a mouth that opens and shuts.'

Moat forced a grin. 'What did he want, Major?'

'He wanted us to organize an air force for him.'

He jabbed at his notebook with his pencil. 'That sure is a story. What did you say?'

'I said, "Not bloody likely".'

He smiled. 'That's the stuff for that murdering devil,' he said. 'They tell me you're an ace, Major.'

'A what?'

'Ace. In the war.'

'Oh!' The Royal Air Force had never gone in for calling successful pilots aces, sniffily considering it all a bit brash and publicity-seeking, something they preferred to leave to foreigners like the French and Americans and Germans, and I was a bit chilly and English with him. 'Yes, I suppose so.'

'Shot down a lot of Krauts?'

'A few.'

'A *lot*, they told me.'

'A few,' I insisted.

'Have it your own way, Major. I also heard you just shot down another – a Mex job.'

'Not "shot down". "Caused to crash". Bit different.'

'I've heard you're down this way to fetch those two girls out of Mexico.'

My heart sank. If this chap was a newspaperman and plastered all over his paper what I was proposing to do, I could see the whole thing falling through.

'I'm not talking,' I said bluntly.

He sat up. 'Aw, hell, Major, c'mon! Give! I got a deadline for tomorrow's paper!'

'Look,' I pointed out. 'Give us a chance. One word from you in that newspaper of yours, and there'll *be* no rescue.'

'Look, Major, I promise—'

'If you want a story, you can have it afterwards. As much as you like.'

'Major, the citizens of the United States have a right to know just what's going on. I can whip up support.'

'It's too late for that now.'

Moat's voice began to grow threatening. 'Look, bud—'

Captain O'Hara leaned over from the next table. 'Sump'n wrong, Major?' he said.

'This chap wants to know what we're intending to do,' I said. 'If he sticks one word in his blasted newspaper about us, that's the end of that.'

'Major, the reading public—'

'Damn the reading public!' I snapped. 'There are lives at stake. We want forty-eight hours of silence, that's all!'

O'Hara rose. 'You'd better come with me, son,' he said to Moat.

Moat jumped up. 'Why?'

'Because I'm putting you under arrest.'

'What the blazes for?'

'Because my job's to prevent the stirring up of trouble along this stretch of border. I guess y'all are aiming to do just that.'

'I have a right!'

'And the United States Government has even more rights,' O'Hara pointed out placidly. 'You're under arrest.'

Solemnly, ponderously, he reached over to the next table where he'd laid his holster with its heavy .45. Unbuckling the flap, he took out the pistol and pointed it at Moat.

'March, son,' he said. He looked at the Sheriff. 'You got a good *calaboso*, Sheriff?'

The Sheriff grinned. 'Best there is.'

Moat had changed his tune now. 'Look, I'm here to get a story and I'm the first here—'

'You'll get your story,' O'Hara promised. 'When it's over. You'll get it all and, since you're the first here, you'll get the best.'

Moat began to back down. Staring into O'Hara's .45, he hadn't much option. 'That a promise?'

'If *you* promise not to try to escape.'

Moat shrugged. 'You got me.' He glanced at me. 'Personal interview?'

'With the two girls, too, I hope,' I said.

'Suppose some other guys arrive?'

O'Hara glanced at the Sheriff. 'They'll join you in the *calaboso*. We'll let *you* out first.'

Moat grinned and now, when I looked at him again and saw he was on our side, he suddenly looked a whole lot better.

'You win,' he said. 'Okay, lead on, Sheriff. I sure hope your jail's more comfortable than a few I've seen.'

Chapter 8

The whole town had heard about Tommy, and they were all out at the field to wait with us for his arrival. O'Hara's men were there with their carbines to keep the crowd back, O'Hara standing by his horse and looking as though he'd been there since the beginning of time – big, square, brown and leathery, as if his vast boots were grafted to the earth.

'You aren't going into Mexico unarmed, are you, Major?' he asked.

'No,' I said. 'I've got a Forty-five.'

He grunted. 'Take my tip, Major. Get the old Colt revolver. It's better. Them automatics are a two-part gun, and we found on Pershing's expedition that they tend to jam when they're dirty. And they're entirely dependent on the magazine, so that if it's damaged or lost, your gun don't fire. The old Colt's a one-part job and she won't let you down.'

'Thanks, Captain. Think you could get me one?'

'I reckon I could, Major. And, if I were you, I'd take along something with a longer range, too.'

'Rifle?'

'They do say that the only thing you're likely to hit with a hand gun's your own foot. If you've got to take a pot at a guy running for cover at a hundred yards, you'd be better with a rifle as well. They're a useful club at close range, too.'

'What do you suggest, Captain?' We were talking to each other like a couple of senior officers in a brigadier's HQ planning campaign logistics.

'Well, *we've* still got the old Springfield and it's too damn long and heavy. Try a carbine. Krag, for instance. There'll be a few about. We used 'em in the Spanish-American war in Cuba and quite a few got sold around when the boys came home.'

'Any in Camarillo, for instance?'

'I've seen some.'

'And you'd undertake to supply 'em?'

'Sure would.' He paused. 'Say, all them medals that newspaper guy mentioned: You really have got—?'

'Yes, I have, Captain,' I admitted. 'It was a bit easier among the flying boys, and I always thought the Poor Bloody Infantry ought to have had a medal even without fighting, just for being there in all that damned mud.'

'They sure did. But—'

'We were the glamour department, Captain. The newspaper people got on to us, and the people at home liked to read about zooms and death dives and all that tripe. Good for morale. And when you got the first gong, so long as you stayed alive the others sort of followed.'

'Yeah—' he nodded slowly '—yeah, I guess.'

As he turned away, I began to look to the north-east and almost immediately I heard the DH. I couldn't see her yet, but in the stillness I knew she was there somewhere in the sky. I'd waited for aeroplanes to return too often not to.

Eventually I saw her low down to the east of Chinati Peak, and almost immediately, someone in the waiting crowd, with sharper eyes than the rest, let out a yell and everybody started to point. Then I saw the familiar dihedral wings of the DH and Slingsby slapped my shoulder. 'You know,' he said, 'I'm damned if I'm not lookin' forward to this little lark.'

'You always were barmy,' I pointed out.

'And you know another thing? It's just the sort of thing to get you another of those damn gongs that so awe the Captain.'

The DH was turning towards the end of the field now, and the smoke was rising from the fire that Lukey and his brother were lighting. I noticed the postmaster and his wife were helping too, so who was looking after the US mail I didn't know.

Dan Tucker stood silently, staring at the sky, his gnarled hands on his hips, completely overshadowing the bent frames of Archie and Snake-Eyes. Evalina was standing by his side, her fists at her mouth again. If she was going to fall for Puddy, who was a born flier if ever there was one, I thought she was going to have to grow more used to him taking off and landing.

The DH came in carefully, because, I guessed, Tommy knew exactly what was at stake and wasn't taking any risks. It touched down as light as a feather and everybody started running towards it, O'Hara cantering alongside, yelling at them to keep back.

As Tommy jumped down, Evalina swung enthusiastically round his neck, then, somewhat more decorously, round Puddy's. I hope to God we bring Charley out safely, I thought. There could be quite a party if we did. I was growing fretful at Evalina's enthusiasm and needed a little myself. It was months since I'd seen Charley and I decided abruptly it was too damned long.

'When do we go?' Tommy grinned.

'Tomorrow morning,' I said. 'Before dawn.'

He nodded cheerfully. 'I'm ready,' he said.

I explained about the aeroplane we'd met and that we had no wish to meet another. He listened quietly then he drew me towards the DH and fished into the rear cockpit. As he hoisted up a sack-covered object, I caught a glimpse of dark gun metal.

'Lewis,' he said. 'The US air force flies SE5s, and there are a few of these about off their top wings because they've started experimenting with double guns through the propeller. I managed to hit on one so I bought it.'

It was a nice thought but I had to tell him that the way we were thinking of doing the job there wouldn't be room for a gun, and its extra weight might be just too much, anyway. He looked disappointed and I could see he was itching to do someone some damage.

'I've got a Scarff ring,' he said. 'I was hoping we could fit it to the rear cockpit.'

'We want everything off the machine we can take off,' I said. 'And then some. We'll spend the rest of the day making sure they're going to fly.'

He nodded. 'She flies one wing low,' he pointed out. 'But I can handle her. What are you flying?'

'I'm not,' I said. 'Puddy's handling the Avro, and Slingsby and I are going in to get the girls out. Slingsby calls us the Camarillo Aerial Striking Force. You and Puddy'll be waiting with the aeroplanes for us to return with the girls. In case it doesn't come off, you'll be taking off and coming back for us the next day.'

We spent the day tinkering with the aircraft, rather, I thought, to Evalina's disgust because she'd clearly been hoping to get Puddy to herself. But Puddy was a dedicated flying man and he was concerned only with the aeroplanes.

We went over every inch of those old machines, checking wheels, control surfaces, engines. They didn't look much, but I thought they wouldn't let us down.

I decided to go to bed early, but first I went to the jail where Moat was sitting on the bunk bed reading an old newspaper and smoking a cigar. I noticed there was a bottle of the Sheriffs 'mouthwash' alongside him and wondered how much it had cost him. I gave him as much of the story as I could and promised he'd get the rest when we got back. *If* we got back, I thought.

'Any other guys arrived yet?' he asked.

'No. You're still the only one.'

I left him looking pleased with himself but whether it was the prospect of a scoop or the Sheriff's 'mouthwash' I didn't know. Back at the hotel, I lay down on the bed in my clothes but I couldn't sleep. There seemed to be an awful lot of this operation still hanging on sheer chance.

I'd obtained a weather report from Lukey's grand-father. He'd lived in Camarillo all his life and from under the peak of his old Confederate *képi* he stared at the sky and the mountains and the faint wisps of mist lying in the valleys.

'It'll be okay,' he announced, sniffing the air. 'Not much wind and that there mist don't mean a damn. You won't want to be puttin' your machine down in an *arroyo*.'

It wasn't professional but I suspected it was probably more reliable for that particular area than anything we could get by cable from somewhere like Washington or New Orleans or Los Angeles in the west. And it was encouraging, and that was something. There weren't going to be any of those crazy winds we'd met when we'd first arrived in Camarillo, so there'd be no major problems to setting the machines down. There'd probably be a few unexpected currents around the Hacienda Las Flores pasture, but we were all experienced and well used to hazards of that kind.

'I still wish we could take the gun along,' Tommy said.

O'Hara arrived with two Krag carbines, two Colts and a Very pistol. The Very pistol was one of the old type, about two foot long and heavy as lead. It looked cumbersome but it seemed a safer bet than smoke from a fire or a mirror flashing morse. Together with the ammunition and two Very cartridges it seemed to weigh a ton.

It was still pitch dark when we reached the field. We were driven out by Dan Tucker in the Franklin, and inevitably Evalina was there to see Puddy off, edgy as a foal and not terribly far from tears. There was a little wind, but not much, blowing dust across the field from the bare *mesas*, and the sky in the east was just showing the first coppery tints of dawn. Someone raised a thin cheer in the darkness then, as torches began to snap on one after the other, I saw the faithful crowd had turned out yet again to see the fun. And oddly enough I didn't for a minute think they were like the crowd that had watched Clint Matthews kill himself. They weren't there for blood. They were solidly on our side and it was surprisingly reassuring.

Then I saw there were already cars parked along the edge of the field and more across the down-wind end where the aeroplanes waited, their headlights shining down its length. An old jalopy covered with names and slogans – 'The Bucket of Trash', 'Fan Ma Brow' – careered past. Judging by the horizontally-striped sweaters and the racoon coats, its owners didn't belong among the bib-overalled inhabitants of Camarillo but had come from somewhere further afield like San José to see the fun and been roped in to help. In the distance, I could see more cars moving into position and a group of people gathering at the up-wind end of the field.

A few minutes later I stood in front of the Avro, one hand on the propeller, watching Puddy do his last-minute cockpit checks. As he nodded I pulled the propeller round to suck in the petrol.

'Contact?'

'Contact.'

Lifting one foot, I heaved and the propeller swung, jerked, then stopped. I tried it again and this time the engine coughed, spluttered and roared, then burst into disconnected burps as Puddy worked the cut-out button. For a moment I wondered if it was as good as I thought it was but, though the engine hadn't started at first pull, that wasn't unusual and I decided this was not time to start worrying. Linking arms with Archie who looked as nervous as ever, even though he was a good six feet from the propeller, Slingsby swung at the DH's prop and the engine roared into life at once. Clint Matthews's mechanic had done a good job on the engine back in San José.

Both machines were quivering now and, as I hurried round to the rear cockpit of the Avro before the usual sheets of flame started issuing from the exhaust, I saw a line of small lights come on at the end of the field. Half the township was there with lamps and torches.

Captain O'Hara had left with his men the night before and by this time, I guessed, was a good ten miles into Mexico to back up Ojarra. I didn't think the five-mile limit would worry him too much.

Puddy looked round at me, then down to the wingtip where Evalina was standing, still pressing her fists into her mouth. He smiled at her – and even at that moment I was pleased to think that Puddy, who'd lost so much in Russia, had probably found something in America to take its place. He lifted up his thumb and the chocks were yanked away and we immediately began to roll forward. The tail came up and then the rumbling ceased. Staring round, I saw a black shape pass between us and the car headlights and knew that the DH was with us.

A quarter of an hour later, heading into Mexico towards the high lands of Chihuahua, I noticed that the stars were already fading. Way behind me the faint lights of Camarillo glowed against the blackness of the land. To the east the horizon was growing more distinct, then I saw the orange-red ball of the sun suddenly appear out of the pink mists and the glow reflected on the dew-wet tiles of a Mexican farmhouse. It wasn't hard to pick up our position and I knew we were somewhere near the unhappy township of Acizpe. The winding road into the mountains was still there and I even saw the old

Ford, picked clean now, nothing remaining except the metal tonneau and the chassis.

Then I saw the pinpoints of a lot of camp fires and just at that moment the sun lifted higher over the hills and I saw horsemen in a valley and smoke lifting from the flames. There appeared to be an enormous number of them and I wondered at first if they were men hurrying to join Guzmán. Then it dawned on me it was Villa's army grouping for his attack on Sabinas in Coahuila. They didn't seem to have moved far, and I could only guess he was clinging to Chihuahua because there he was on home ground and could rely on sympathy, support and provisions.

I thought I recognized the country, then I spotted the scattered wreckage of the Jenny strewn along the top of the canyon where it had crashed. It looked like a collection of old sticks and pieces of wood and it was amazing that its crew had survived.

I took a good look round. Perhaps I *had* destroyed the whole of the Mexican Air Force, but perhaps also I hadn't and there was more of it lurking around somewhere, and this time perhaps it wouldn't be just a Jenny but a Camel or a Fokker, because aeroplanes from the European war were turning up in the strangest places and one might conceivably have reached Mexico.

But there was no sign of anything and, if nothing else, the wreckage had placed our position. I tapped Puddy's shoulder and pointed.

Then, as he turned, not far to the north I spotted the men who'd appeared when we'd destroyed the Jenny, a troop of fifty-odd men in bus conductor's hats and uniforms, cantering along with their machine-gun cart, their rifles slung across their backs. They were kicking up a lot of dust and I just hoped that Villa's Dorados didn't spot them. Villa didn't like people in smart uniforms, whoever they belonged to.

I also hoped they didn't turn up near Las Flores, because we'd have enough to handle with Guzmán's men. I was still thinking about it when I realized the sun was just touching a low white building on the hillside and I could see smoke.

'Las Flores!'

I leaned over, tapped Puddy's shoulder and pointed.

'There's the landing strip. And, by God, Ojarra's in position! I can see smoke and it's drifting down the field. You can go straight in as soon as Tommy's caught us up.'

Circling high over the plateau, we waited for Tommy whose machine was just two slanting bars against the sky.

'Okay. Cut the engine.'

Switching off, Puddy swung in a silent curve beyond the end of the pasture and began a long slow glide in to our destination. It was faintly eerie to be sitting up there above the land, with no sound except the wind wailing through the wires and rustling across the wings. The sun was just peeping over the mountains now and touching the wingtips with gold. It was as if the machine was on fire, the doped fabric throwing back the light from its rippling surface. Faintly behind us I could hear the low growl of the DH's Liberty engine, throttled well back, as she came in behind us for her landing. The wind seemed to sough through the wings as we rustled through the air, sliding, it seemed, down a long straight chute towards the earth.

I could see the Hacienda Las Flores about half a mile from the field and there appeared to be no lights or any sign of life. I decided that Esplenderoso Guzmán, damn his black soul, had obviously committed the first and most heinous sin of any military man. He'd posted no sentries.

This was it, I told myself. This was *it*.

–

I had my eyes glued so tightly to the *hacienda*, watching it intently for any sign of life, that I hadn't noticed how close we were to touching down. The first thing that drew my attention to it was the vacuum-like feeling when the aeroplane checked and lifted as the updraught from the side of the *mesa* held her – devoid of power with the switched-off motor – hanging over nothing. For a second, I thought we weren't going to have enough air left to make it, but then, just as she was about to stall into the valley, Puddy dropped the nose quickly and we just slid over the edge of the drop to touch down on the sparse grassy surface of the little plateau. The rumble of the wheels was reassuring and comforting and I gave a sigh of relief.

I glanced round. Sharp against the sky I could see the shallow double V of the DH's wings as she slipped into place to touch the earth a little to one side. Thank God for good pilots, I thought. There was a lot you could do with people who'd taken the trouble to learn their job. During the war I'd seen all sorts and I'd noticed that the careless, the indifferent and the over-bold never lasted long. There was a saying that there were old pilots and bold pilots but no old bold pilots, and there was nothing more true. Having gone through the campaign in South Russia with these three men, I'd have trusted them anywhere.

The Avro rolled to a stop and I caught a whiff of wood smoke as the little fire that had been lit at the end of the field by Ojarra's men wafted down on the breeze past the cockpit. Hitching at the Colt that I'd strapped round my waist and slinging the Krag rifle – fastened behind my back not with good military web strapping, but with a piece of clothes line borrowed from Young Lukey's mother – I slipped from the cockpit to the wing and down to the ground. The DH slid in alongside us and rolled to a stop just ahead. The dark shadow of Slingsby joined me as the DH turned and began to head back at once down the field towards the down-wind end ready for take-off.

'If anything goes wrong and we don't get back,' I shouted to Puddy, 'tell Tommy we'll contrive to be here every morning. But if he sees no smoke, no reflecting mirror or Very light, he's not to land.' I pointed upwards. 'Tell him to be up there every morning at dawn until we turn up. After a week, he's to give it up and contact every government official he can and persuade them to send the United States Army, Air Force and Navy in after us. Okay?'

Puddy waved. 'Okay.'

We grabbed the Avro's tail, lifted it and spun her round so that she was facing down-wind ready to head back to the limit of the field to turn into wind.

'Contact?'

'Contact!'

Slingsby heaved on the propeller and the 80-horse Mono burst into life at once with a crackling snarl that would have wakened the dead. Blipping the engine, Puddy zigzagged away from us until he became a shadowy shape moving towards the end of the field.

Almost at once I heard a shot. As I swung round, a light went on in the Hacienda Las Flores.

'Let's hope they think we've just come for a look-see,' I said.

As I spoke, I heard a hiss in the darkness and swinging round, my hand on the Colt, I saw a dark shape topped by the tall cone of a sombrero. I was already dragging at the Colt in a panic when a voice came, soft and urgent.

'*Señor!* Brazil – Carmen Encarnación Brazil. I am from Señor Ojarra.'

He signed to me and we flopped down among the rocks with him. He spoke reasonable English and it was possible to understand.

'You are the *señor* who destroyed the aeroplane with your guns?' His grin was reassuring.

'Not with guns,' I pointed out.

He stuck out his two forefingers and worked his thumbs. 'Tat-tat-tat – boom! – crash!' He gave a gust of laughter.

'Whose was it?' Slingsby asked.

He shrugged. 'Obregón's? Carranza's? Murguía's? Villa's? *Quién sabe?* Nobody knows who anything belongs to in Mexico today.' He came back to the job in hand and gestured. 'Señor Ojarra is on the north-west,' he said. 'The *arroyo* curves round that side and he is waiting for the first sign of your arrival. As soon as we are in position, I am to fire my revolver and then he will start shooting.'

'Fine. Can you lead us there?'

'*Si, mi Capitán*. We will use the *arroyo* to reach the *hacienda*. This way they will not see us. We will come up by the corral where Guzmán has his horses. Can the *gringas señoritas* ride?'

I still cherished a picture of Charley out with the Quorn which she'd sent me in France. At the bottom she'd written, 'The one on top's me.'

'One can,' I said.

'It will be enough.' Brazil had a hoarse voice as if he had a cold and it seemed to make every announcement he offered a sinister utterance. 'I have saddled and attached head ropes to four of them. We shall use them to get back to the aeroplanes. I think we shall be in a hurry.'

'Too right we will,' I said. 'Okay. Let's go. We can't have much time.'

Brazil gestured. 'It is impossible to see the top of the *mesa* from the *hacienda*,' he said. 'But they will have heard and it will not be long before they send someone down to investigate.'

'You're tellin' me,' Slingsby said.

The din of the Avro's blipping engine had sounded like bursts of machine-gun fire and, if Guzmán had thought that was what it was, then more than likely he'd bolt. Time was of the essence.

Following Brazil, we dived into the dark *arroyo.* It was full of morning mist and the smell of the dust we stirred up as we slithered down the steep sides among the scree on our backsides. Running along it, Brazil gestured and we started to climb again. Getting out of the valley was more difficult because the surface was loose, but we made it in the end; and as we flopped to our knees at the top, panting, Brazil hoisted a murderous-looking pistol from his belt. As the light caught him, I saw he was literally festooned with ammunition belts, while we'd crammed only a few spare rounds in our pockets for the rifles. He looked villainous, but I suspected that like most Mexicans he enjoyed blazing away with his weapons and probably wasted half of what he'd carried.

'The *señor* is ready?' he asked.

'Go ahead,' I said.

The pistol roared and almost immediately a barrage of firing came from beyond the *rancho.* It sounded encouraging and exciting and, heaven help me, I felt my blood surge. I'd always felt in Europe and Russia that I was never a true warrior because every time I'd ever gone into a fight I'd cringed from it as you'd cringe from a cold shower. But when I was in it, with the blood racing and the enemy there in front of me, with no time to think, I'd always found a tremendous sweeping excitement that had made me realize how it was that the Light Brigade had managed to charge down that long valley at Balaclava against the opposition that had been mustered against them. They'd probably been too excited to be properly terrified.

As he stuffed away the vast pistol, Brazil gestured to us and we ran forward, keeping in the shadow of a dry stone wall that ran in a crooked line towards the tumble-down barn-like structure.

O'Hara's Very pistol was as long and heavy as a horse pistol and by no means the sort of thing that was normally carried strapped to the waist. During the war they'd only been brought out when needed and, running with it, with the pistol and rifle, and with pockets heavy with ammunition, was like running in full kit.

By this time more lights had gone on in the house and I could hear rifles popping. I decided at that moment that there seemed an awful lot of them, and their owners all seemed very wide awake. There was a hole in the back of the barn and I struggled through after Brazil, banging my shins on an ancient wooden plough such as had probably been used centuries before by the Aztecs. I could hear shouts in front of me now.

'There is the door, *señor*,' Brazil said. 'I think if we do this quietly, we might not even be noticed with what is going on at the other side.'

The rattle of musketry was coming in ripples from the far corner of the house. Considering he had only six or seven men, Ojarra was certainly making them sound like a whole troop of cavalry and I could just imagine his namesake, O'Hara, down in the valley, probably picking up the sound on the wind and fidgeting by his horse, itching to do something for the good old USA. At least, I thought, we seemed to have picked reliable people on our side because everybody seemed to be doing what they were supposed to do – and at the right time.

'*Preparado, señor?*' Brazil said, and I nodded.

He made a sweeping gesture over his head with his arm, as if he were summoning a whole brigade of troops to follow him instead of just two lunatics, and set off running bent-double for the house. Fetching up alongside him, our backs to the wall close to the plank door, we waited for his signal. At a nod, I swung round, tried the latch, found it didn't lift and kicked out as hard as I could. The door burst open and inside, staring up at us in horror, I saw a young Mexican no more than seventeen or eighteen years old, who was on his knees, plucking bullets from an ammunition belt. Before he could move, Brazil was astride him and I saw a knife flash. The boy tried to cry out, but the call ended in a sickening gurgle I knew I'd remember all my life, as his throat was cut.

Flinging the body aside, Brazil gestured at the inner door as much as to say 'Your turn, *señor*,' and I jumped forward. As I reached the door, another Mexican appeared, dressed in a city suit with one of the scout hats O'Hara's men wore. But, like Brazil, he was festooned with belts of ammunition. He seemed as startled as I was, but I was quicker to recover. I kicked him in the stomach and down he went. Brazil grinned and his knife flashed once more.

Slingsby was looking a little green. Most of the fighting we'd ever done had been with aeroplanes and machine-guns at a good distance from our victims, and this close cut-and-thrust stuff with knives was unnerving.

Beyond the inner door was a long hall that opened out, through another door, to another room where I could hear the roar of rifles. Guzmán and his band seemed to be well occupied with Ojarra, and as I heard a yelp of pain, I realized that Ojarra's party had accounted for at least one man. Since we'd accounted for two more, that only left twenty or so. A mere nothing, I thought, trying to cheer myself up to forget the hollowness in my stomach. Then glass tinkled and something thunked into the ceiling above our heads, and plaster dusted down. It seemed to be time to move on.

We knew exactly where the room was where we'd seen the girls wave and we'd already carefully studied a plan of the house that Ojarra had supplied. Bounding along the corridor, we wrenched at a door. From inside a voice called, '*Quién es?*'

'Guzmán!' Brazil said.

As a bolt clicked back and the door opened, we were inside at once. Facing me was a thick-set man, all pomaded moustache, yellow teeth and vicious brown eyes. As he lifted a revolver, Slingsby swung his rifle and, as the butt connected, he went down with a crash.

'Bolt the door!'

As we turned round, I saw the girls. They were sitting on a bed covered with dirty blankets, their wrists tied together by a rope that was passed through the iron uprights of the bedhead.

'Martin!'

Charley looked tired and grimy and her hair was untidy, but the delighted grin she gave us showed she hadn't lost her spirit. The other girl was smaller, darker – black-eyed and as French-looking as the Arc de Triumphe – but she was pretty, too, even if she looked as tired and dirty as Charley.

As Brazil's knife flashed, the two girls were free and Charley was in my arms in a second, clinging to me as if she'd never let go. The other girl looked a little bewildered for a moment then, deciding to follow suit, she flung herself at Slingsby.

'I say,' he said. 'Never expected this.'

There was no time for affectionate greetings. Any moment now, the men in the room at the end of the corridor would suspect something had happened and come to find out. I moved to the window and looked out. Brazil appeared alongside me and flung the shutters back, but as I was about to climb out to help the two girls through there was a hammering on the door.

'Quick, for God's sake!'

I jumped through the window to help them out. Charley didn't stop to ask questions but jumped through so fast after me she almost knocked me flying. Before I'd recovered Dominique Duellin had followed her, knocking me to my knees. Brazil came afterwards, until I was swamped by people. As I struggled to my feet, I saw Slingsby cock one leg over the sill, then I heard the crash of the door bursting open and he calmly lifted his revolver and fired. There was a yell and he slipped to the ground. 'Four,' he said. 'Only leaves a couple of million.'

Someone was shooting at us from the window of the room at the end of the corridor and we had to fling ourselves down on the rocky earth behind a straggling bunch of cactus. Then I heard running feet and shouts and another blaze of musketry from Ojarra's direction.

The shooting stopped but the running feet didn't, and I became worried that someone was getting between us and the horses. Grabbing Charley's hand, I started to bolt for the out-buildings, but she dragged her hand free and ran beside me.

'Easier,' she panted. 'Never did go much on this strolling hand-in-hand business.'

We half-fell into the shadows of the barn. Quite clearly Guzmán had realized we'd escaped with his prisoners, because bullets kept whacking into the mud of the *adobe* walls, gouging out great chunks. Picking our way through we headed for the corral, but as we climbed the fence I realized what had happened and what those pounding feet had meant. The gate was open and the horses were just bolting to the end of the mesa. We hadn't a cat in hell's chance of catching them. Mexican ponies, like Texan cattle ponies, were as active as cats and jumpy as crickets, and unless they were securely penned up or hobbled they were impossible to catch.

There was nothing for it but to make the journey to the aeroplanes on foot.

As we left the corral, a shot whined past us and I saw two men running towards us. Brazil dropped one in his tracks and as the other, heading towards me and Charley, passed the shadows where Slingsby was crouching with the French girl, I saw him rise up and swing the Krag again like a club. The Mexican's feet lifted from under him and Dominique gave a little shriek, while Charley turned and pushed her face into the angle of my neck.

'Oh, God,' she said in an unsteady voice.

'Come on,' I said brusquely. 'We've no time for squeamishness, old love. It's them or us.'

'Yes.' She swallowed and fought down her fears. 'I'm all right. Just don't mention it, that's all.'

Even without the horses, we'd got away from the house and I thought we'd actually made it, but as we dropped into the *arroyo* and began to run along it I heard the slow tat-tat of a machine-gun. At first I thought it was Tommy and that he'd somehow managed to mount the Lewis without us noticing it, after all. Then I realized the sound came from the other side of the corral. Lifting my head I saw two men with a cart and caught the flickering blue flame from the muzzle – and I realized we weren't the only people who could work out plans.

Guzmán had suspected something all along – probably from the moment he first saw me over the place in the Avro – and had mounted the gun on wheels so it could be moved about easily: he was now firing it at long range towards the two aeroplanes.

Chapter 9

The sun had come up now, and I could see the Jenny's wings glinting in the light and the blue puffs of smoke from the exhausts. Tommy and Puddy had very sensibly kept moving, and the two aeroplanes swung and swerved about the down-wind end of the field to make hitting them harder.

'Think we dare make a dash for it?' I said.

But even as we put our heads up, the Mexicans spotted us and the gun swung so that bullets chipped the dust and stones along the lip of the *arroyo.*

I stared at Charley and then at Slingsby. 'For God's sake,' I said. 'We can't risk the girls!'

The French girl had started to weep in noisy hysterical sobbing. I guessed she was tired, probably hungry, and certainly in a highly emotional state after being a prisoner for several days with no knowledge of how it all might end. I'd once seen Charley in France, taut-mouthed and courageous after dealing with the most appalling hospital cases, suddenly dissolve into weeping because I'd said something nice to her.

For a moment or two she tried to comfort the French girl, speaking softly to her, but when it brought no reaction, she simply swung her arm. The crack as the flat of her hand caught the French girl's cheek was like a pistol shot. Dominique flopped back from her knees on to her behind, her legs straight out, her expression startled.

Charley helped her up. 'Sorry, old thing,' she apologized. 'But you can't go off like that, you know.'

To her credit, Dominique got hold of herself and shook her head. 'No,' she said. 'It is *trés mal élevé*, I think.' She managed the ghost of a smile. 'It is also not very British.'

Charley's manner was deliberately brisk. I could just imagine her in later life, head of the Red Cross or something, bullying people to do things her way, but I knew it was chiefly to hide her own fears.

'What happens now?' she asked.

'For the moment,' I admitted, 'I'm damned if I know. It seems we're a bit stuck.' For the first time I looked at her and sheepishly leaned towards her and kissed her.

'Thanks,' she said. 'Wondered when you were going to get around to it.'

'Are you all right? Did they harm you?'

'Not they,' she said spiritedly. 'That chap Guzmán was polite enough. Perfect gent. Even lent me a comb. But the chap who cooked soup for us was a different cup of tea altogether. Tried to kiss me. He got his soup in his face straight away. He was lucky it wasn't a hatpin in his eye. I had one with me because I was still wearing a hat when they grabbed us. I was just waiting for a chance to use it to escape, as a matter of fact, when you turned up.'

'Good old Charley,' I said.

She gave a sudden shudder and leaned weakly against me and I realized it wasn't bravery that had kept her head up so much as Bartelott-Dyveton-Sykes pride. It just wasn't done in her family to show too much emotion.

'Frightened stiffs actually,' she said and I saw her lip was trembling and her eyes were full of tears. 'Oh, Martin, it was awful. Thank God you came. I knew it was you the first time I saw the aeroplane.'

I kissed her again, pretty brusquely because there seemed to be no time to waste in showing affection. Guzmán's machine-gun was sending short bursts in our direction and any attempt to reach the aeroplanes was going to be not only dangerous but probably fatal. I just hoped Tommy and Puddy had guessed what had happened.

That they had was made apparent even as I thought of it. The machine-gun was probably managing to hit them at times and I heard the motors roar. As I saw them lift up beyond the edge of the *arroyo*, rising into the sky, bright against the sunshine, my heart thumped down in my stomach.

They circled above us for some time, trying to see us, and we tried waving but they showed no sign of noticing. It was impossible to use the mirrors we'd brought to do any heliographing. For one thing they were too small and for another the sun was in the wrong position.

'How about the old Very pistol?' Slingsby suggested.

'If I fire it they'll land, thinking we'll be able to reach them, and with that damned machine-gun up there they'll probably end up dead. I think we've just got to hide and hope they come back tomorrow.'

The problem was solved for us by Brazil. He touched my arm and pointed down the *arroyo.* There were men and horses there and at first I thought that somehow Guzmán had got behind us. But it was Ojarra and I realized then that the shooting at the *hacienda* had stopped.

Ojarra had a bandage round one hand and one of his men had his arm in a crude sling.

'I have also lost Eulalio Gutíerrez,' he said. 'There are only six of us now. But we have spare horses. I think we must get away from here quickly and hope that Captain O'Hara will be in the valley waiting for us.'

The aeroplanes were still circling above us, but it was clear it was impossible up there to make out what was happening below. The sun was still low, the *arroyos* full of blue shadow, and it was impossible for them to see a thing. And they couldn't stay there for ever, because they couldn't take a chance on not having enough juice to return to Camarillo. They had to live to fight another day, and at least Charley was no longer in Guzmán's blood-stained hands.

Horses were brought up and I pushed Charley aboard. She was wearing a dirty, stained dress but she sat in the saddle as if she'd been born there, and I was pleased to see that Dominique also appeared to know what to do with a horse. Seeing us all mounted, Ojarra signalled to us to follow and swung his horse down the *arroyo*.

'There are too many for us,' he said. 'Another twelve of them appeared while we were waiting. But I had promised, so I stayed.'

Point in your favour, old son, I thought.

Stones clattering beneath the horses' hooves, we moved into the *arroyo*. It was a long fissure in the land, separating two flat-topped plateaux, the bottom filled with dust, stones, dry withered plants and patches of sere brown grass. We must have made at least ten miles down its length and I began to have hopes we'd make it all the way to Captain O'Hara waiting on the plain. But the *arroyo* wound and twisted, and as the crow flew I doubt if we covered much more than six or seven miles. But, at least, I decided, we were that far away from Guzmán.

I was just congratulating myself when Ojarra lifted a hand and the horses bunched, nose to tail, as he reined in. Silently, he gestured. Somewhere ahead we could hear horses and the click of metal shoes on stones. Then we heard voices speaking in Spanish.

'Guzmán!'

Gesturing quickly, Ojarra directed us into a cut-off from the valley and we moved to our right, down the narrower fissure. I was scared we'd end up in a cul-de-sac, trapped there until Guzmán's band could round us up like cattle, but I suspected Guzmán was also growing worried, too, now. He'd been holding prisoner two foreigners and, whether what we'd done to rescue them fitted in with international protocol or not, there wasn't much Guzmán could claim in his defence.

With Obregón now on the threshold of power, there were hopes of law and order returning to

Mexico, and people like Guzmán would be hunted down like wild animals. Everybody knew now that Villa was anxious to accept a pension and a parcel of land in return for retirement, and I had a suspicion that Obregón might even call on *him* to settle this troublesome gnat on the border that was disturbing the tranquillity of the newfound peace. It seemed to me that Guzmán would find it important to capture us if only to remove all traces of his guilt, because without doubt the British and French governments, when they finally got moving, would also demand satisfaction.

There was no sign of the aeroplanes now. I knew they'd turned north and could only hope they'd be able to think of what to do next, because I certainly couldn't.

The sun was high now, beating off the ochre walls into our faces. Slingsby and I had come dressed for flying in thick sweaters, jackets and coats: we began to discard our clothing bit by bit until we wore nothing but breeches and shirts, and even that was hot.

Charley's hair by this time was damp with sweat and Dominique was sitting limply in the saddle. Ojarra was grim-faced and whispering incessantly with Brazil. I knew he was worried. Guzmán's band had proved to be bigger than he'd expected and he was anxious to get back to his home. Mexican hatreds were intense and feuds were normal, and I knew he was concerned to get his family and the families of his men over the border to safety until Guzmán was removed and the chance of bloody vengeance erased.

It was too hot now to keep moving in the sun, so Ojarra suggested we find shade and shelter. There wasn't much, because the sun was barely past its zenith. But we found a little and stayed there as the sun passed over the edge of the *arroyo* and the shadows grew longer. Ojarra had water and provisions so we decided to eat while we could. Slingsby had kept whistling between his teeth in his mad fashion, but as it grew hotter with the afternoon and the dust lay on his lips he had to give up. He did his best with Dominique, however, trying hard to cheer her up.

She was small and fine-boned – a bit, I remembered, like Puddy's sister Olga, whom we'd left behind in Russia. She had enormous dark eyes with small dark shadows under them like so many Frenchwomen, and she was quiet and serious, but somehow Slingsby kept managing to raise a smile.

A thought occurred to me and I turned to Charley. 'What in God's name made you come up through Mexico?' I said. 'Why on earth didn't you come by sea?'

She managed a smile and swept her hair from her eyes. 'I thought you'd think of that one sooner or later,' she said. 'It was Father.'

'Oh, no!'

Charley's father could hardly be called the brightest of the Bartelott-Dyveton-Sykeses. He'd served bravely enough through the war, but there was something missing from him somehow, a flaw in his make-up, and he'd never been able to hang on to his money so that he'd borrowed from the rest of the family until Charley had squirmed with humiliation. After the war he'd taken his wife and Charley to the south of France, thinking it would be cheaper to live there, but of course the way *he* lived it wasn't and Charley had bundled him home pretty quickly. The offer of a job with the Cowdray petroleum company in Veracruz just before I'd left Russia had been the last I'd heard of him.

'What happened?' I asked. 'Did he get the push?'

'No.' She gave a short dry laugh. 'In fact, the poor lamb got promotion. They said he had to go to head office in Mexico City now that the revolution's over, so off he went. The poor dear actually made terribly sure that everything was safe for me and there was no fighting going on. After all, it made sense, because at one period you couldn't stick your nose outside your door in the main street without getting it shot off. We reached Mexico City without the slightest trouble, and I was quite prepared to go by rail up to Tucson and come back along the border to El Paso, but it seemed a devil of a long way, and then we heard rumours that Villa had thrown his hand in and decided to be a *pacifico.* Everybody we asked – the railway, the embassy, the government – all said it was safe to travel via Torreon and Chihuahua. It was going to save days, and after all it was months since I'd last seen you. We decided to chance it. Nobody thought that lunatic Guzmán would cut the railway line and land us in Camarillo.' She smiled. 'Even *that* might have been all right if you'd arrived ten minutes earlier to meet us. I bet he wouldn't have kidnapped us if you'd been there.'

'By God, he wouldn't,' I said. 'How about Dominique?'

'Same as me. Her father's in the French embassy in Mexico City and they wanted her safely in the States. She's got an uncle in Louisiana and they'd enrolled her for the university in New Orleans. Like me, she thought it would be quicker to go via Chihuahua instead of going all the way to Tucson or Los Angeles.' She stared at me and suddenly her eyes filled. 'Oh, Lor', Martin,' she sighed. 'What a mess! What's going to happen now?'

From time to time Ojarra sent one of his men down the *arroyo*, but they all brought back the same message. Guzmán's men were across our escape route. Then he tried the other way and we found, as I'd feared, that they were there, too, waiting under a cliff that hung over the bones of some lost steer that had wandered down there and died.

The sun was low now and the depths of the *arroyo* were growing into purple shadows. Suddenly it was cold and, as I made Charley put on my sweater, I noticed that Dominique was wearing Slingsby's. I put on my jacket, thankful I hadn't thrown it away when the sun was at its hottest as I'd been tempted to do, then Brazil made a fire in a cave and boiled water for coffee. As Charley and the French girl huddled together, talking, I drew Slingsby to one side.

'Any idea where we are?' I asked.

'Haven't the foggiest,' he said. 'Couldn't be hell, could it? It's been hot enough.'

'What the blazes are we going to do? It looks to me as though we've jumped out of the frying pan into the fire.'

'There's always Captain O'Hara.'

'He hasn't the slightest idea where we are.'

Slingsby shrugged. 'Well, Tommy and Puddy won't give up easily,' he said. 'I dare bet Puddy's thinkin' hard round this one. *He* wouldn't leave you here. Not after you fished him out of Bolshevik country last year.'

'But, like Captain O'Hara,' I pointed out, 'they don't know where we are either. And even if they did, you could hardly land an aeroplane here.'

Slingsby stared about him. 'It *is* a bit narrow, since you mention it,' he agreed. 'Got any ideas?'

'One or two. None of 'em much use. What do you think's up top?'

He lifted his head. 'Flat plain,' he said.

'With grass?'

'Bit. Like that pastureland we landed on. Sparse. A few stones.'

'Think an aeroplane could land on it?'

'You thinkin' it might?'

'I'm wondering if we could find a landing strip up there, clear it of the worst rocks and sit up there to wait for Tommy and Puddy to come back.'

'Go on, old boy. Sounds interestin'. More than possible, shouldn't wonder. You always were one for bright ideas.'

'It would mean one of us – perhaps both of us – going up there and having a look. It'd mean climbing up. In the dark, I imagine, because otherwise Guzmán will spot us. We could recce the place, shift the rocks, gather wood and grass and have a bonfire ready for the morning.'

'Think Tommy and Puddy would see it?'

'They'll certainly be looking, won't they? They'll go back to Las Flores first, of course, but if we're not there they'll wonder where we are and start sniffing around. A fire would attract them and I've still got the Very pistol.'

'Amen to that and thank God.'

'If they spot smoke they'll come down to investigate and when they're near enough I can let off a Very light. They'll realize the landing strip's okay. We can make an arrow with stones and light a fire to indicate which way to land. They'll know then we're here and how to get in. We could all cram into the planes. Two in each rear cockpit.'

'Sounds all right – if it works. What about Ojarra?'

'I'd thought of that one. I reckon Ojarra's only staying with us now because he's promised old Tucker. I bet if we weren't here, he'd think of saving his skin – and probably do it, too.'

'Right.' Slingsby hitched at his breeches. 'When do we start?'

–

I was right about Ojarra. He was fidgety and nervous and was still with us only because he was an honourable man and had promised Dan Tucker that he'd do what he could to help.

'But I have seven *muchachos*, *señor*,' he pointed out grimly. 'And my wife is not strong. I must get them to safety.' He shrugged. 'I must also think of my men. They have families, too.'

I explained what I was thinking of and he agreed to help. 'I will post men further up the *arroyo*,' he said. 'We can hold them off here for ever—' he paused '—or as long as our water and food last out.'

'How long would that be?'

'Two to three days, *señor.* No more.'

'We'd better start tonight. Then we can be up on top at daylight and prepare for the planes. If nothing comes, we'll come back after dark.'

He nodded and I went to tell Charley what we had in mind.

'Can I come?' she asked.

'Not this time,' I pointed out. 'We don't know what we're going to find up there. Perhaps even Guzmán. Besides, it might be covered with boulders and quite impossible to fly into. If it's worthwhile, though, we'll all go up there tomorrow.'

'I wish you didn't have to leave us behind,' she said. 'I'm such a rotten coward.'

We sat by the fire for some time. There was no point in leaving too soon. There was a small breeze teasing the dust into little whirls and I guessed that on the flat *mesa* above it would be as cold as the very devil.

As it grew sharper, I felt Charley moving nearer. 'Mind if I come a bit closer,' she whispered. 'I'm frozen.'

'All you want,' I said, putting my arm round her. 'Here, have the jacket.'

'Don't be silly,' she said. 'I'm not *that* cold. To be honest it's just that I *feel* like being a bit nearer, and you'll need the jacket yourself when you get up top.'

'Think you'll be all right tomorrow until we can get back to you?' I asked.

'Sure we shall.'

'How about Dominique?'

'She'll be all right. She'd better be.'

'Does she scare easily?'

'Bit more easily than me, I think. I was always too stupid to get very scared. The only thing that scared me was when I thought of you flying. It still scares me.'

'Think I ought to give it up? I would if you wanted me to.'

'Not on your life,' she said spiritedly. 'You'd die without aeroplanes. You'd manage fine without me.

You'd probably be sad if I disappeared but you'd get over it. But if you were told you could never fly again, you'd curl up and die.'

'That's not true,' I said indignantly.

'You know jolly well it is.'

And when I thought about it, I did.

'All the same,' I said, 'it's not fair.'

She managed a little laugh and gave me a peck on the cheek. 'Got you where it's tender,' she said. 'But I don't mind. I suppose any girl has to accept these things and the last thing I'd ask you to do would be to give it up and become a green-grocer.'

'Green-grocering's safer,' I pointed out.

She smiled. 'I'm sure it is. But I'm not sure that green-grocers are quite so interesting. Believe me, I like my Martin the way he is.'

We talked in whispers for a long time until I fell asleep. When Slingsby woke me up, I noticed that Charley was curled up against me.

'How about it, old lad?' he asked.

'I'm ready.'

Ojarra was waiting by the fire. He nodded without speaking, and we set off without waking Charley or the French girl. He'd found us the beginnings of a path and it was easy at first. But the slope grew steeper and seemed to go on for ever so that my legs were aching after the first half hour. Occasionally we dislodged stones which went bouncing down into the *arroyo*, and I hoped to God Guzmán wouldn't hear them and guess what was causing them. We'd stuffed some of Ojarra's dried meat in our pockets and carried a half-full water bottle, but it didn't seem much and it had to last us the whole of the next day. We also carried the rifles tied tightly across our backs with Lukey's mother's clothes line, and had the revolvers in holsters round our waists. In addition I had the Very pistol, so that it was hard work climbing, and all the time the equipment we carried kept catching on rocks or dried trees that grew out of the slope.

The last fifty feet seemed to be almost sheer, but the moon was full now so we were able to manage. As we flopped over the lip at the top, we lay on our faces gasping for a while, and when I lifted my head it was like looking at those pictures of the surface of the moon people liked to draw in popular magazines, though how they worked it out when nobody had ever been there I could never imagine.

The cold blue-white light made everything silvery, and it looked so bleak and bare my heart sank. Then, the more I stared at it, the more I cheered up. There were a lot of stones, but none of them was big and I reckoned we could clear a landing strip. There were also a few dried bushes that we could pull up and gather for a fire, and a strong breeze blowing which would mean that a landing into it would be short and sharp.

'I think we can do it, Sling,' I said.

He nodded. 'I think we can.'

'How about starting straight away? After all, it's still night time and I shouldn't imagine Guzmán's lot will be coming up here – if they're coming at all – until daylight.'

I gestured. At the far side of the flat stretch of grassland, there was another small escarpment, this time no more than thirty feet high, leading to yet another, slightly higher, plateau. This second plateau was small and had a butte rising out of it like the spire of a church, but the escarpment leading to it was pitted with holes where the wind had eroded the soil.

'Somewhere to hide,' I pointed out. 'Shade during the day. Let's get cracking.'

The huge moon made things easy. There were a lot of small stones scattered across the plateau and we walked from one end to the other about twenty feet apart, picking up the biggest and throwing them to the side or rolling them out of the way. When we'd finished, we turned round and came back, doing it over and over again.

'Can't be many left,' Slingsby said, 'and my old dogs are beginning to ache.'

'Just a few more times,' I insisted.

'Oh, Lor', what it is to have friends who're pernickety!'

'We wouldn't want the aeroplanes to burst a tyre,' I said. 'I reckon we ought to keep it up as long as we can. We can sleep all day tomorrow.'

Slingsby didn't argue and we spent the rest of the night moving backwards and forwards along that narrow little plateau, tossing stones aside until our backs and legs ached. By first light the place looked picked clean, and we started to lay the biggest rocks at one end in the shape of the letters F and S with a crude plus sign between them – F + S. If Tommy and Puddy didn't realize that they meant Falconer and Slingsby they were a lot dimmer than I'd ever thought them.

'Pity we haven't any whitewash,' Slingsby said. 'You know the old sayin': "If it moves, salute it. If it doesn't, paint it white." A little of the old RAF bull and a bucket of whitewash and we could have this place lookin' like the station warrant officer's hut. All it would need would be a few little posts and loops of rope all nicely painted, and a sign, "RAF, Mexico." I'd stand guard. I've got a rifle.'

'Shut up,' I said, 'and build these letters up. Bigger and higher so they'll throw a shadow when the sun comes up.'

'Yes, sir! Of course, sir! Bigger and higher, sir!'

We were still working when the sun rose and I was delighted to see the piled stones casting thick black lines. Any aeroplane flying over them ought to spot them quickly enough. If not, the Very pistol would soon draw attention to them.

Leg-weary and jaded, we were just about to head for the escarpment and lie in the sun to warm up a little before finding a hole to sleep in when Slingsby grabbed at my arm.

'Listen!'

My head swung round. Aeroplanes! And I knew exactly *which* aeroplanes, too!

We saw them coming from the north-east, two narrow lines with a dot in the middle, the way they'd always looked as they'd come over the trees in the early morning after the dawn patrol, or in the evening light with the sun glinting on the wings as they'd returned from a last look at the lines.

They were heading straight for us and Slingsby grabbed my arm. 'Fire the Very,' he yelled.

I'd actually got the thing out and pointed at the sky, with my finger on the trigger, when I lowered it.

'Go on, man! Pull it!'

'No!'

'Why not?'

'For God's sake,' I yelled back at him in a fury. 'We haven't got the girls! We can't go off without the girls.'

Slingsby saw the point and became silent, and we watched the two aeroplanes fly low over us, heading south-west. In the distance we saw them circling near the Hacienda Las Flores and heard the drum-drum of their engines. They seemed to go on for ever but, after an hour, we realized they were heading back the way they'd come, north-east towards the border and Camarillo. We watched as they passed overhead, suddenly cold and hungry and dog-tired. They'd shown no sign of seeing the letters we'd so elaborately fixed up and I suddenly began to wonder if they would.

Silently we watched the aeroplanes vanishing into the distance, the sun catching their wings as they grew smaller.

'Think they saw us?' Slingsby asked.

'I'm damn sure they didn't,' I said.

'Think they will?'

'They will if we light a fire and send up a Very light. I've got two.'

'I hope you're right,' Slingsby said in a deflated voice.

I nodded. I hoped so, too.

–

It was as scorchingly hot through the day as it had been freezingly cold during the night. We crouched in what shelter we could find in a small cave in the escarpment which was filled with small bones, as though some carnivore had used it as a lair. We slept for an hour or two and woke to find the heat like an oven. Putting my head out, I was staggered to find how many stones we'd missed on the landing strip we'd prepared. With daylight and under the piercing sun, there seemed to be hundreds of them left. Wearily I roused Slingsby.

Like me, he was hollow-eyed, grimy and bearded by this time.

'Oh, no,' he said, when I told him what I'd discovered.

'It can't be!'

'Look for yourself!'

'Can't we chance it?'

'Would *you* have chanced going into a fight in France or Russia with your guns not cleaned?' I asked. 'No, you damn well wouldn't! That's why you're still around to tell the tale. With aeroplanes you don't take chances, and some of those stones out there are big enough to burst a tyre.'

He nodded and crawled out into the sunshine. The brassy ball was high in the sky by this time and the glare made us squint. In the distance we could see the barren land of Mexico stretching away to the north in its flat ridges and valleys and, in the distance, we could see the blueness of the mountains beyond the border.

Seared by the heat, parched and leg-weary, we began our trek up and down that stretch of burnt-out grassland. It seemed to grow longer every time we covered it. Perhaps my first impression, one of shock, had made it seem worse than it really was but there were some fair-sized stones, all the same, that we had to get rid of. Finally, well into the afternoon, our mouths dry, our food and water finished, we stumbled back to our cave in the escarpment and lay down in the shade.

'Think it's all right now?' Slingsby asked.

'If we've time, we'll keep going over it,' I said. 'Perhaps the girls'll help. We can't take chances, Sling.'

After that, we didn't talk much. We hadn't the energy and the baking heat dried our throats. Towards the end of the afternoon, we heard a flurry of shots beyond the lip of the *arroyo* and then silence. There weren't many and I felt that it was only Guzmán's boys trying to reach Ojarra and failing; but even so, despite my conviction, I could hardly sit still until the moon came up.

'Think we ought to go now?' Slingsby said.

'No,' I said. 'They'd spot us the moment we started down the cliff face. And, even if they're rotten marksmen—'

'Which, thank God, they are!'

'—they could still pick us off like sitting ducks from the main *arroyo.* At the very worst, they could make us lose our grip and I don't fancy doing a hundred foot nose-dive to the bottom. We can't do anything now. If it *was* Guzmán breaking through, then we're already too late. If it wasn't, we're best to hang on.'

But as I became silent I found myself praying that it *wasn't* Guzmán breaking through. Then I tried to imagine what Charley and Dominique Duellin must be feeling. They'd have wakened to find us gone, and they'd seen neither hide nor hair of us for almost twenty-four hours. As far as they knew, Guzmán had murdered us.

As the sun went down it started to grow cold and, in no time, after the heat of the day the reaction set in and we started to shiver. We were already tired; and hungry, too, now; and our teeth were soon chattering. As soon as we saw the glow of the moon coming up beyond the lip of the land we started to grow restless, and hid the rifles and the Very pistol for when we returned; then immediately the lower rim of the silvery orb was clear we both stood up without a word, mutually accepting that this was the moment to move.

It was harder work climbing down than climbing up, especially since we were growing tired now and careless. Once, Slingsby went sliding past me, dislodging scree and small stones. My heart in my mouth, unable to do a thing to help, I called out to him, then I saw him fetch up against a spar of rock over a sheer forty-foot drop. There was a long silence then his head lifted.

'Jolly nearly crash-landed,' he said.

As I reached him, he edged gingerly away from the drop to join me and we continued down. Then it was my turn. A stone I'd had my foot on crumbled away and I found myself hanging by my fingers until I could find another toe-hold. I tried not to look down but it was impossible to avoid it as I searched for a handy ledge for my feet, and the distance down made my stomach squirm within me.

We slid the last twenty or thirty feet on our behinds and arrived at the bottom of the *arroyo* in a shower of dust and small stones, me with a hole in my breeches. Charley dragged me to my feet, clinging fiercely to me.

'Martin,' she said shakily, 'I thought I wasn't ever going to see you again!'

'I bet you've thought that often in the past.'

'Yes, I have. But this time it seemed worse.'

Ojarra appeared through the shadows. He looked tired and grim.

'What was the shooting?'

'They tried to edge closer, *señor.* We stopped them. It was nothing.'

I explained what we'd done at the top of the cliff and Ojarra managed a grim smile. 'I think perhaps we shall make our escape after all, *señor*,' he said.

'I hope so,' I said. 'We're going straight back, to be ready for tomorrow morning. We'll need ropes to help the girls. Can you let us have one?'

Ojarra smiled. 'Two, *señor*. Two are always better than one and there are two *señoritas*, no?'

I turned to the girls to explain what we had in mind. They were looking scared now and suddenly they seemed quite exhausted – and very dusty and dirty, because it had been hot in the *arroyo* – hotter than on the plateau above – and there'd been no water for washing. Charley refused to leave me, clinging to my side wherever I moved.

'Sorry I'm being such an ass,' she apologized, and I grabbed her by the shoulders and kissed her. It was a dry dusty sort of salute, but it made me feel better and it seemed to help her.

Dominique stood watching, a small forlorn girl with her long dark hair over her shoulders, her enormous black eyes scared. Slingsby put an arm round her waist and she gave him a grateful look.

'I think we shall now have to be brave,' she said.

'I think you will,' Slingsby said. 'Think you can do it?'

'It will be difficult, you understand, but I think I shall manage.'

I described what we intended and I saw Dominique look up at the cliff face nervously. Ojarra stood watching silently, his men sitting on the rocks behind him.

'What about you?' I asked him.

'We shall be all right,' he said.

I wasn't sure what he meant but I had to take him at his word.

I stared up at the rock face and my heart sank. It seemed to tower away up into the sky for ever. My legs were already weary and I wasn't any too sure I was going to be able to do it again.

Ojarra made the decision for me. 'First you must eat,' he said.

One of his men made coffee with the last of the water and we ate what was left of our food. Ojarra kept only a little back for the journey he proposed to make. When we'd finished, I began to rise but he pushed me down.

'Sleep, *señor*,' he said. 'Two hours. It will be enough.'

What he said made sense. I glanced up again at the cliff face. I had no wish to be caught up there in daylight, but he knew as well as I did that neither I nor Slingsby were in any state to make that climb back so soon after coming down.

I didn't argue but lay down on one of the horse blankets. Charley sat beside me, holding my hand. I woke up to a grip on my shoulder, starting me awake. Charley was still holding my hand. I looked up at her.

'Hello,' I said. 'How's Charlotte Margaret Caroline Bartelott-Dyveton-Sykes?'

'All right,' she replied. 'How's Mark Martin Falconer?'

'Not so dusty.'

I was cold and, as I sat up and flapped my arms to warm myself, a cloud of dust, silvered by the moon, jumped from my clothes. We both looked at each other and smiled at what I'd said.

'How do you feel?' I asked.

'I'm game.'

'Thought you would be. We'd better start.'

I glanced at my watch. It was just gone midnight. We had a good four hours before daylight and that was ample.

'Let's go,' I said.

We hitched at our belts and adjusted the revolvers, then we rolled two of the blankets up and tied them with a length of *reata* from Ojarra's saddle.

'We can hoist 'em after us,' I said. 'It'll be easier with a rope.'

I shook hands with Ojarra and every one of his men. They even managed to produce smiles. They looked ragged and dusty, and the man with the wounded arm was looking pretty ill by this time.

'How are you going to get away?' I asked.

Ojarra shrugged. 'I think when the aeroplanes come,' he said, 'Guzmán will take his men up there to see what is happening. That will give us our chance.'

'Right. We'll be off. Good luck.'

'And to you, *señor. Vaya con Dios*.'

I had thought the climb up the cliff face was difficult the night before, but this time it seemed never-ending. I was tremendously tired by this time and desperately hungry despite the meal we'd eaten, and I was worried sick for the two girls. Slingsby, the lighter of the two of us, went first, and though he'd never done any mountaineering to my knowledge he soon discovered how to use Ojarra's *reata*. Hitching one end to spurs of rock, he tossed the other end down so that I could loop it round the waists of the girls for him to help haul them up. The climb was difficult for them because, when they'd been snatched up by Guzmán in Camarillo, they'd been wearing light shoes and their feet were already cut and bruised. They'd long since removed their torn stockings and Charley, indifferent to conventions in the best Sykes tradition, had hitched her skirt up and tied a knot in it to leave her knees free.

'Great-Aunt Charlotte would never approve,' she said cheerfully.

Slowly, painstakingly, we moved up the cliff face, first Slingsby, then Dominique, then Charley, then me. Slingsby seemed to have recovered his energy more than I had, and at times my heart was in my mouth as I watched him pulling himself upwards among the rocks. Half-way up we found a ledge and rested on it to get our breath back. We'd been warm from climbing, but on the ledge the breeze found us and we were soon half-frozen. Charley's fingers slipped into mine.

'Almost there,' she said.

I glanced up. There was still a long way to go and the top part was the worst.

In the end it was the cold that drove us on. Slingsby gave a little sigh, which was all he allowed to show

how tired he was, and set off again. A few moments later the *reata* came snaking down and I started to fasten it round Dominique's waist in the way Ojarra had shown us, so it wouldn't slip or tighten. As she began to move upwards, Charley stood alongside me.

'Think we'll make it, Martin?' she asked.

'Yes,' I said bluntly.

'It's jolly romantic, isn't it, when you think of it?' she said. 'Imagine what the papers'll say: "Beautiful – well, fairly beautiful – Heiress Rescued By Handsome – well, fairly handsome – Officer".'

I grinned at her. It was a weary grin but she returned it, still full of spirit.

'It's the sort of thing we used to read about at school,' she said. 'With a torch under the blankets when we were supposed to be asleep. I used to love those magazines they printed for romantic girls. *Peg's Paper* and *Betty's Booklet*. The maids at home used to adore them, and when no one was looking I used to sneak them out of the kitchen to read in bed. Mother would have called it lowering myself to the level of the kitchen staff. Actually, I thought the kitchen staff a lot more interesting than some of Mother's friends.'

The end of the *reata* dropped alongside us with a soft rustle of the rope against the stones. I touched Charley's hand.

'Lift's arrived, Ma'am,' I said.

As I tied it round her waist, she gave me a peck on the forehead. 'Fourth floor please, porter,' she said.

'Shall I have the luggage sent up?'

'If it's not too much trouble, that would be kind.'

I tugged on the rope and, as she started upwards, I slapped her behind. 'See you in the ball-room,' I said.

Her voice floated down. 'I'll save you the last dance.' There was a faint giggle. 'Martin, it's like eloping. All it wants is Father at the top with a shotgun.'

As I waited for the rope to return, I became aware how tired I was. I'd had about four hours' sleep in three nights and climbed twice up the cliff and once down, with nothing to eat but a few scraps and practically nothing to drink. In addition to all that, I'd spent both nights and most of the intervening day on my feet. My legs suddenly felt like lead.

The last stretch was agony to my muscles but, oddly enough, it wasn't me but Charley who almost disappeared to the bottom. Just as we reached the top, her foot slipped and, as she tried to save herself, the light shoes she wore failed to support her and she wrenched her ankle. Slingsby heaved on the rope as her feet slipped away, and I heard him yell.

'Dominique!'

The French girl's head appeared as they both began to heave on the rope, while I reached up and tried to push Charley's toes back into their holds.

When I reached the top myself she was sitting on the rocky ground, crying. 'Oh, Lor', Martin,' she wailed. 'I think I've sprained my ankle! I'm so sorry, I'm so sorry, I'm so sorry!'

'It doesn't matter,' I said. 'We're there now.'

'But it might hold you back! You must leave me!'

She was weeping copiously now, and Dominique started to cry in sympathy. They were dog-tired and their emotions were played out. They'd been through too much.

'It doesn't matter,' I said, kneeling by Charley. 'We don't have to do any more walking.'

'You must save yourself.'

'Don't be damn silly!' I snapped, and she stopped crying abruptly.

'Sorry, Martin,' she said in a small humble whisper. 'Sorry I made an ass of myself.'

'You've got a job to do,' I said. 'You've got to look after Dominique. I don't think she's quite as tough as you. You've got to keep her going a bit longer.'

'Yes. Of course. Sorry. Didn't realize.'

Immediately she became efficient, collected and cool. Limping across to Dominique, she put her arm round her, pushed her hair from her face and kissed her gently. Slowly the French girl began to recover.

'What now, Martin?' Charley asked.

I indicated the low escarpment at the far side of the little plateau. 'There's a cave over there,' I said. 'You might be able to snatch a bit of sleep.'

'What about you?'

'Things to do.'

We got them into the cave and watched them roll themselves in the blankets, then we stared down the stretch of grassy land again.

Slingsby gave me a tired grin. 'We're goin' to go over the blasted place again, aren't we?' he said.

Chapter 10

Without a word, we started walking down the length of the plateau again. I was worried sick there might be a single rock we'd missed because even one could be enough to wreck our chances.

The breeze was still blowing steadily from the west so, while there was still some moon, we built the landing T in the way they were used on aerodromes back home, to show the direction for landing and take-off. With the pile of brushwood at the end of the runway, I felt sure we'd be able to make it.

Exhausted by the climb, the two girls were already asleep but I daren't lie down myself because I knew I was so tired I'd fall asleep too, and then we could miss the aeroplanes when they came searching for us.

Instead I started walking up and down that damn stretch of runway again, still looking for stones, not because I expected to find many now but to keep myself awake. Slingsby joined me, but after a while he shuffled to a halt.

'Try and sleep,' I said.

'Daren't. Might not be able to wake up.'

As I set off again, he began to stumble after me once more. By this time I could see the first hint of daylight showing, and I was staring anxiously at the sky. Then I heard it. The first faint hum of an aeroplane engine.

'They're here,' I yelled. 'Wake the girls! It's got to be quick!'

While Slingsby set off in a weaving, exhausted run to the cave, I grabbed up the Very pistol and hurried towards the pile of brushwood we'd built. As the girls emerged, Slingsby came stumbling back.

'Where are they?'

We stood staring up into the sky, peering into the growing daylight. Then Slingsby pointed. 'There!'

But his voice was hollow with disappointment because the aeroplanes were miles away to the north.

'They'll never see us!' he yelled furiously. 'They're too far away!'

'Hold it,' I said. 'Don't panic! Not yet! They've got to come back!'

The aeroplanes droned on until they were mere dots in the sky, and we saw them circling in the distance near where the Hacienda Las Flores lay. They'd arrived slightly to the north of the previous day's course and were looking for smoke and a Very signal; and it suddenly occurred to me that if they weren't looking where we were they might not see anything.

They remained near the *hacienda* for a long time, flying backwards and forwards until I knew their petrol must be running low; then, finally, I saw them turn and start to head north again.

'Stand by that fire, Sling,' I said, reaching for the Very pistol.

Charley was standing just behind me, her hair blowing in the wind, her eyes dark-ringed with tiredness, her face dirty where the dust had smeared on the perspiration of the previous day. The aeroplanes were heading towards us now and I nodded to Slingsby. As the first puffs of smoke lifted and began to drift down the field, I realized there was something wrong with the DH, then, over the drone of the Avro, which was nearer, I heard the Liberty engine coughing.

Slingsby had heard it, too. 'Complicates things a bit,' he said, his face gaunt with weariness.

'Never mind. Get the smoke going. I'm going to send up the Very light.'

As the aeroplanes approached, I raised the pistol and pulled the trigger. The Very light shot into the air in a long curving white streak, then there was a puff of smoke and a brilliant red ball hung in the sky. For a moment I thought it hadn't been seen, but then the Avro turned in our direction. The DH, however, continued in a straight line, heading north, its engine still coughing.

As the Avro flew towards us, we all started jumping up and down and yelling, kicking up the dust with our feet as we did so. It passed above us, the Mono making its curious snarling crackle as it passed, but then that machine also changed course northwards and continued steadily after the DH.

As it grew smaller, the sound of the engine becoming fainter, we stopped our antics, deflated and suddenly desperately weary.

'They've left us,' Slingsby said.

'Puddy saw us,' I pointed out. 'He must have. He came back.'

'Then why the hell didn't they pick us up?'

'Perhaps the DH was having trouble.'

'Then that sinks us, because the Avro can't pick the lot of us up.'

'It can take the girls,' I pointed out. 'And they'll send O'Hara in for us. They know where we are now.'

'How do you know?' Slingsby said quietly. 'Nobody gave any sign.'

'He *must* have seen us,' I said doggedly. 'He must have.'

As I turned, I saw the two girls standing together, Dominique haggard with tiredness, Charley, with one arm round her shoulder, standing on one leg, the other foot, minus its shoe, held just above the ground. I felt I had to say something, because the silence as the engines died away was agonizing. I indicated her foot.

'That hurt?' I asked.

'Bit.'

'I think you'd better get back in the cave again. Rest it. Sun'll be up soon and it'll be hot.'

Charley said nothing for a while, then she looked me straight in the eyes. 'Will they come back?' she said.

'Of course.'

'You sure?'

'Yes.'

I wasn't sure at all really, despite my insistence that we'd been seen, but I could hardly say anything else.

We helped them back into the cave and Slingsby and I sat down to keep watch. We were both desperate for sleep now, but we daren't close our eyes. Anybody who's tried to waken exhausted men knows how impossible it is, and I'd seen officers in Russia actually kicking their men to bring them back to consciousness and still failing.

Slingsby looked at his watch and glanced at the sky. 'Goin' to be hot,' he said.

'Yes.'

'Daren't go to sleep, Martin.'

'No.'

'Perhaps we'd better inspect the landin' strip again. You can hardly go to sleep standin' up.'

'Better collect more brushwood, too,' I pointed out. 'We've used all that lot.'

I lost all count of time as we stumbled about gathering twigs and brushwood and dried grass and placed them near to the dying fire.

'Wonder if Guzmán spotted the Very light,' Slingsby said suddenly.

That was something that hadn't occurred to me and I stopped dead. 'Think he might?'

'It went up a long way. They do. They're intended to be seen over long distances. He might well have.'

I gestured. 'Let's get the rifles,' I said.

We slung the rifles on our backs and began to wait again.

'Listen!'

Slingsby lifted his hand.

It was an aeroplane engine and by the sound of it, it was the Avro. My heart leapt and I looked at Slingsby delightedly.

'There it is!'

The elongated dot hung low in the sky to the north, growing more clear with every second. Then the sound grew into the crackling snarl of the Mono and finally the Avro swept towards us, and this time I could see a hand waving.

'Stoke the fire!' I yelled.

As Slingsby piled the fresh brushwood and dried grass on the dying embers and the smoke puffed out again, the Avro roared over the top of us and began to swing at the far end of the field.

'Get the girls,' I yelled and Slingsby began to run in a shuffling stumble that showed how leg-weary he was.

The aeroplane was settling now, dropping lower. Puddy was taking every care, turning into wind as slowly as he dared to shorten his run. The wheels touched and it was only then that I remembered that he was landing on young Lukey's motor-bike wheels. So much had happened since we'd mounted them, I'd completely forgotten them. As the Avro's tail skid touched, the dust puffed up and began to trail behind as she slowed, the comma tail wagging as she came up the field, her nose into wind.

But, as the machine came level with me I heard a shot and the whine of a bullet, and for a moment I looked round, dazed with sleeplessness, wondering who the devil was shooting. Then I spotted a conical-shaped sombrero on the lip of the *arroyo* and knew at once that what Slingsby had suggested had happened. Guzmán had spotted the Very light and had found a way up to investigate. I dropped down in the sparse grass and worked the bolt of the Krag. As I pulled the trigger, I saw dust leap into the air within a couple of feet of the sombrero and it vanished abruptly.

'Get the girls aboard!' I yelled.

The aeroplane had swung round now to face down-wind ready to head back towards its take-off point.

'Trouble with the DH,' Puddy yelled. 'Fuel leak. Tommy tries to repair it. I must take you two at a time!'

'You'll have to be bloody quick,' I yelled back. 'Splendid Ben's just over there about a couple of hundred yards away.'

'I know. I see them climbing up as I pass over last time. I am almost out of fuel and cannot waste time. There are rifles and ammunition in the rear cockpit.'

Slingsby climbed up and tossed out a couple of rifles, and ammunition which had been stuffed into a sack. There was so much of it, he could hardly lift it.

'We can waste it like the Mexicans now,' he said.

We pushed Dominique into the rear cockpit. She looked terrified and was half-blinded as her hair was whipped across her eyes by the slipstream. Another shot came from the edge of the *arroyo* and I snapped one back, standing upright. It went nowhere near the marksmen, I'm sure, but it made them keep their heads down.

Charley was standing by the aeroplane, looking bewildered.

'What about you?' she demanded.

'They'll come back for us. Get aboard.'

She stared. 'No,' she said suddenly, her voice rising. 'I'm not going!'

This wasn't a bit like Charley. 'Get aboard,' I yelled furiously.

'No! I'm staying. If you're not going, *I'm* not going. Let somebody else go.'

'Get aboard, dammit!'

'I'm staying with you.'

'You're not,' I roared. 'Get aboard, blast you!'

She stared at me for a moment, then she nodded meekly. 'Yes, Martin. All right.'

I pushed her roughly into the rear cockpit after Dominique and slapped the fuselage alongside Puddy.

'Get going,' I yelled.

He waved. 'I come back.'

'Make it quick, for God's sake!'

Between the burps of the blipping engine, I heard a faint wail of 'Martin,' from Charley, then the aeroplane was moving, jolting towards the down-wind end of the strip, the wings rocking as it went. Another bullet whined over and I gave Slingsby a push. He was staring open-mouthed at the Avro as though he'd never seen anything so beautiful in his life.

'We'd better get under cover!'

As we started to run for the cave, the Avro's comma tail wagged and she swung round to face into wind. I started to pray, because it was only a short run and the Avro had three up. Then the engine settled to its dry-throated snarl and she began to jolt towards us. The tail came up and I saw daylight under the wheels.

'They've made it!'

There was one more heart-stopping moment as she passed over the *arroyo* and I saw her falter as the updraught caught her. She seemed to hesitate and for a second I thought she was going to plunge out of sight to the rocks below, then Puddy caught her and she lifted steadily upwards, followed by a whole hail of bullets from the other side of the strip.

'Masterful way with girls you've got, old boy,' Slingsby said.

Certainly Charley had seemed a little awed.

'Practice,' I said. 'Always at it.'

It was only as we reached the cave and flung ourselves down that I realized what we were in for. Now, I thought, comes the tricky bit. It was going to take Puddy the best part of an hour to get back to Camarillo, perhaps an hour to refuel and check, and then an hour back.

'Three hours,' I said.

'What?'

I gestured across the strip. 'That's how long we've got to hold these boyos off.'

Slingsby grinned. 'Well, we held off Kaiser Bill's hordes, and the whole of Trotsky's Red Army.'

'There were more than two of us then,' I pointed out.

As I spoke, there was a flurry of shots from the other side of the strip, and we heard the bullets clinking against the rocks by the cave and whining away into the air. A sombrero appeared. I drew a bead on it and, as I pulled the trigger, I had the satisfaction of seeing it jump into the air.

'I think I got one,' I said.

Then, to our surprise, I saw horses. First one, then another, until there were about two dozen milling around just below the lip of the plateau. Somehow they'd found a route up for them.

Whistling in his usual ear-piercing way through his teeth, Slingsby was still struggling to unfasten the knot that held the mouth of the sackful of ammunition.

'Get that damn thing open!' I snapped. 'And quick! The blighters are going to try a cavalry charge!'

'What!' Slingsby whirled. 'Good God,' he said.

He thrust a handful of ammunition at me and gripped his rifle.

'Look,' I said, 'I don't know what they're up to, but for God's sake don't bring anybody down right in the middle there.'

'If he gets in the way of one of my shots, that's his rotten luck.'

'Luck be damned,' I pointed out. 'We spent half last night and the night before clearing that blasted strip of rocks. You know how big a horse is. We don't want one sprawled right across the landing strip. It's not that wide.'

He stared at me and grinned. 'Got you,' he said. 'Silly of me not to think.'

'Wait until they turn off or something. You know what we want.'

'Right.'

'Here they come!'

Suddenly the horsemen swept up over the edge of the plateau, two dozen men in wide sombreros on dusty-looking ponies. In spite of everything they were a splendid sight, festooned with ammunition, colourful and curiously out-of-date, galloping down the far side of the strip by the edge of the plateau, obviously wondering just where we were and what to do.

'I think now's fairly safe,' Slingsby said, pulling the trigger.

One of the horses went down with a crash in a cloud of dust and flying stones and lay stretched out, flailing about, wounded and unable to rise, its nose searching the dust, lifting it in little puffs with its own blood and foam.

Slingsby frowned. 'Never did like gettin' horses involved in shootin',' he said, and as he pulled the trigger again the horse gave a convulsive jerk and lay still.

'Where's the rider?' he demanded.

'Other side of the horse, I think,' I said. 'Better keep an eye on it.'

By this time, the other horsemen had reached the far end of the strip and were wheeling to return. Yelling and screaming, firing their rifles with more abandon than skill, they came thundering back towards where the dead horse lay. In the lead was a big man dressed in a suit and bowler hat. He was showing off a bit, and I even wondered for a while if he were Splendid Ben, because his horse was caricoling on its hind legs along the edge of the *arroyo* as if he were trying to prove how close he could get. I pulled the trigger while the animal had its forefeet in the air and it came down heavily, then pitched forward to its knees and rolled sideways with its rider over the edge of the plateau.

We heard the crashing and the long-drawn-out scream as they disappeared, then there was silence. I thought I'd hear that yell for the rest of my life in nightmares, and the other riders seemed as shocked as I was because they all halted, milling around, a perfect target. Slingsby didn't seem to have been quite so affected as I was, because he pulled the trigger again and one of the saddles emptied, then the remaining horsemen bolted off the plateau, followed by the man whose horse Slingsby had hit, running in a stumbling shuffle, holding his leg, until he was grabbed and whipped out of sight.

For a long time neither of us said anything, then Slingsby spoke and I knew he'd felt the same as I did.

'Lor',' he said slowly.

The Mexicans had vanished now, but I didn't think for a minute it was the end of them. I poked my head out and crept among the rocks to get a better view up and down the length of the escarpment above us. Seeing a tall sombrero move among the rocks at the top end, I gestured to Slingsby.

'Think we'd better move further out,' I said. 'Into the rocks. Just in case the blighters try to get above us on the escarpment.'

He glanced at the sky. 'It's goin' to be hot,' he said. 'No shade.'

'We've got to chance that. Puddy ought to be back in two or three hours or so.' I indicated a group of large boulders just to the right of the cave and twenty feet away from the escarpment. 'There,' I said. 'You go first. I'll cover you.'

'Right.'

'Got the ammunition?'

'Yes. Better take the Very pistol as well, just in case.'

'Right. Get cracking. Ready?'

'Yes.'

'Go!'

As he ran I saw two or three heads bob up, and I started firing as fast as I could work the Krag. The heads ducked out of sight quickly, all except for one which lifted higher, then its owner stood boldly upright and started to run towards us as if he hadn't the patience to wait any longer. I dropped him as he ran, then a whole burst of firing whacked bullets into the escarpment round me; a stone flung up by a bullet hit me above the eye and opened my eyebrow. At first I thought I'd been shot. It had flung me on my back with the shock and I lay among the rocks, half-blinded by blood, then I felt myself all over, realized I had all my senses and the use of all my limbs and scrambled dazedly to my knees.

'Brat! I'll cover you. Come on!'

Ducking as low as I could, I grabbed the rifle and started to run. Slingsby started firing as I had, keeping down the heads opposite, and as the return fire came I took a flying dive to drop alongside him in the dust. I landed on a stone and at first I thought I'd broken a rib, and lay there gasping, then as I struggled up Slingsby turned and saw the blood. His jaw dropped.

'You hit?'

'No. Stone.'

'Bet it hurts.'

'Like hell.'

'Have the devil of a headache tonight.'

I wiped away the blood with my sleeve and crouched against the rocks. The sun seemed to be scorching suddenly and the sky was as metallic as a gong. To the waist our shirts were dark with sweat, and I looked at my watch. Less than an hour had passed and I began to wonder if we really could hold out for another two hours.

The Mexicans made several attempts to get closer but we kept driving them back, then, gasping in the heat, wishing like mad we'd got some water, I spotted them trying to sneak along the top of the escarpment behind us.

'Watch that side,' I said and pulled the trigger.

I saw dust jump and the Mexicans bolted back towards the main group.

'Hope Puddy makes it back soon,' Slingsby said. 'Don't fancy another night here.'

'He'll be back, don't worry.'

Burnt, feeling charred under the pitiless sun, a layer of dust over the sweat on our faces, our thick clothes clinging to our weary limbs, mouths open as we gasped for breath, we seemed to wait for aeons of time. The blood on my face dried so that it seemed to pull at the skin and I began to get a headache. Then once, in the heat, I felt myself dropping off to sleep and jumped to wakefulness to see one of the Mexicans regarding me from the top of the escarpment. I shot him as he ducked for cover and saw the sombrero rolling as he vanished from sight.

'Don't think that one'll come back,' Slingsby said.

'No. How much longer?'

'Any time now.'

But the time dragged by on leaden feet and the need for sleep grew worse.

Slingsby's head jerked and I knew he'd been dozing off. 'Nearly asleep there,' he admitted. ''Strewth, I'm hungry. I could eat a mangy pup.'

He'd never been behind the door when appetites were handed out. 'You always could,' I said. 'But there's nothing left, so you'll have to manage.'

His cracked sun-dried lips moved in a thin smile. 'We could always eat each other,' he said.

'It's an idea.'

'Bags first bite.'

'Not likely. The way you go at food, I'd never get a chance.'

It was silly banter but it helped to keep us awake. Then Slingsby started whistling through his teeth again.

'I never noticed before how much you do that,' I said.

'Do what?'

'Whistle between your teeth.'

He looked surprised. 'Do I? I didn't know.' He glanced at his watch. 'Can't be long now.'

'No. Not long. And we seem to have that lot across there tamed for a bit.'

But as we spoke the Mexicans decided to try another charge and they came over the lip of the *arroyo* yelling. We drove them back once more, and as they vanished I realized why they'd come: I could hear an aeroplane. Probably more alert than I was, they'd heard it first and decided they'd better do something before it arrived.

It was the Avro again, dropping lower towards the plateau to circle beyond the end of the runway.

'They're bound to try a rush when he's stopped and we're climbing aboard,' I said. 'You go first. I'll cover you. Then you cover me from the cockpit while I run for it.'

'Other way round,' Slingsby said. 'With that eye, you'll never be able to hit anythin'. Probably even shoot me. *You* go first, and pass the rifle to Puddy. Let *him* cover me.'

It made sense. I didn't argue.

Then we saw the De Havilland. It was low in the sky a long way behind the Avro, and we let out a croaking cheer.

'Tommy's made it, too!'

'Four's better odds than two,' Slingsby said. 'But the same still applies. You first. I'll have the Avro. You go for the DH. If we decide now we shan't waste time arguin'.'

'Who's arguing?'

'Well, it stops us gettin' scared, then.'

'Who's scared?'

Slingsby grinned. 'Me,' he said.

The Avro was still circling, waiting for the DH to draw closer, then, as it drew alongside, Puddy started to drop towards the end of the plateau. Immediately there was a tremendous burst of firing from the Mexicans, some of it directed towards us and some towards the aeroplane. Fortunately it was as wild as ever, and though we heard the bullets whining over us none of them came near us.

The Avro was hovering, seemingly motionless, over the edge of the plateau, caught by the updraught, then Puddy dropped the nose and she slipped in, touching down within twelve feet of the edge, and started to roll towards us, rocking on the uneven ground, the wide double-strutted wings the most beautiful things I'd ever seen. As she approached the DH dropped down behind her.

I wanted to cheer as the two aeroplanes rolled towards us; but my mouth was too parched and I felt too tired, anyway, so I just crouched behind the rocks and watched them with narrow eyes under dust-caked eyelashes. The Avro made a half-circle, ready to head back the other way, then just behind it the DH took a big sweep round and dropped into place, too – as it happened, nearer to us than the Avro.

'Go!' Slingsby yelled.

Without arguing, I started to run. A couple of bullets kicked up the dust near me, but then I was on the lower wing and scrambling into the rear cockpit. I caught a glimpse of Tommy's face grinning at me and, in my dazed state, realized he was yelling something.

'What?'

'The gun! Use the gun!'

Then it dawned on me that the Scarff ring in the rear cockpit had been mounted with the Lewis Tommy had brought from San José. It looked like the sword of the Lord or something to me just at that moment.

'I fitted it while they were working on the fuel feed,' Tommy yelled. 'Thought we might be able to use it.'

'By golly, we certainly can!'

There was a pan of ammunition already in place and the gun was held in the fore-and-aft position with a loop of rope tied to the Scarff ring. Alongside, held in place by another length of rope, was a second pan of ammunition. It was hardly the load of trouble the machine had carried in wartime, but I reckoned it would be enough.

Grabbing the gun, I unhooked the loop of rope and swung it round; then, pressing the trigger, I directed a long burst along the edge of the *arroyo.* It sent all the sombreros that were bobbing about there ducking out of sight and Slingsby started to run, dragging the sack with the remains of the ammunition.

As he disappeared out of sight into the rear cockpit of the Avro, it started to move away at once. For a moment he seemed to be upside-down because I could see more of his feet than his head, but he finally reappeared right way up, waving and clasping his hands above his head like a boxer. Then a flurry of firing made him duck and fish behind him for his rifle and I had to send two more long bursts towards the Mexicans to make them stop.

Then to my horror I saw a cart appear on top of the escarpment, followed by a troop of horsemen. They wore uniform and bus conductor's hats and they were setting up a machine-gun. They'd seen all the air activity from below and come to join in, too. They were the same government troops we'd seen before – *somebody's* government troops, anyway – and they'd clearly decided they were going to get the *gringos* who'd destroyed their air force. Doubtless they knew nothing of the abduction of the girls; they could only see Guzmán's men doing precisely what they were intending to do themselves, and they were joining in to help.

The machine-gun cart was in position now and the gun was swinging towards us. If that thing got going it was probably the finish for us. We'd done everything we could, but machine-guns were just too much.

By this time the Avro was moving quickly down to the end of the field, and as Tommy opened the throttle of the DH to follow I saw a whole swarm of the uniformed men appear on the escarpment in a perfect position to shoot at us. I swung the gun and pulled the trigger and several of them dived for cover. But, as I pulled the trigger again, the gun died as the pan of ammunition emptied. We were virtually helpless.

Then, almost as if I were watching a Wild West film, from behind and to the left of the soldiers I saw a whole swarm of horsemen appear – hundreds of them, it seemed. At first I assumed they were more reinforcements and that we hadn't a chance against all that firepower, not even in an aeroplane; then I realized that they wore sombreros not uniform caps and that they were charging along the top of the escarpment firing their rifles – not at us, but at the soldiers and Guzmán's men. They came over the lip like maniacs and I saw three horses go down, but they were already among the machine-gunners, shooting or slashing with machetes, and both the soldiers and Guzmán's men began to turn tail and run, only to be shot down as another swarm of men appeared from the other side of them.

I was still gaping at this unexpected help when I saw a magnificent black horse appear from among the confused *mêlée* of men and animals. In the saddle was the broad-shouldered, moustached man we'd met in Acizpe. He was handling the animal as if he were part of it and I saw him raise his sombrero and start to wave it wildly.

'Villa!' I yelled. 'For God's sake, it's Pancho Villa!'

I was already holding the new pan of ammunition and the Avro had turned and was swinging into wind. As it began to race past us in the opposite direction for take-off, Tommy ruddered the DH round and opened the throttle. I waved frantically back at the splendid ugly figure on the horse, and he grinned and gestured with his rifle.

'*Viva Villa!*' The yell burst out of me instinctively, not because I admired his special brand of villainy but because he'd been as good as his word. He'd produced almost his last *golpe terrifico* before he vanished into legend, and he'd done it for us simply because he'd taken to us. '*Viva Villa!*' I screamed, waving like mad. '*Viva el Gran Capitán!*'

It was then, as he became hidden by the tail, that I saw Esplenderoso Benavenides Guzmán for the first time. I knew at once it was him. He was high-nosed, lean and handsome and was dressed in a black traditional *charro* suit decorated with silver filigree, with silver buttons down the front of his jacket and along the slit in his wide trousers. On his head was a black sombrero, silver-edged like his suit and studded with *pesos.* He was mounted on a magnificent bay, with a scarlet saddlecloth decorated with black, and he was racing towards us across the landing strip, waving a rifle.

There was no question about who it was. He matched his name. Splendid Ben. Gorgeous Gus. And in some mad, prideful need to show off, he was racing forward on a horse to do battle with an aeroplane moving towards him at fifty miles an hour.

What urge forced him forward, I don't know. Perhaps it was disappointment at seeing us slip away. Perhaps it was sheer frustration at being finally defeated by his old enemy, Villa. Or perhaps it was even some sort of suicidal desire to destroy himself. He must have known it was all over and that this was his final gesture. As a Frenchman had once said to me, 'A gesture is not much really, you understand, but sometimes it can be very moving.' And, much as I'd hated him this *was* moving, the final contest between ancient and modern, the very limits of the range, a horse against an aeroplane: if we hit him it would not only kill Guzmán but probably us as well, because the weight of that huge horse would shatter the airscrew and smash the wings.

Tommy hadn't seen him. He was staring forward, concentrating on holding the aeroplane straight for the take-off, and Guzmán was thundering towards us away on my left. This time there could be no help from Villa or his men because the aeroplane was between him and Guzmán and any firing would have hit us. As it was, a few stray shots thumped into the tail, and I knew that in a moment it was going to be impossible even for me to stop him; as he headed across our path, the wings would be in the Lewis's field of fire and I wouldn't dare shoot for fear of hitting our own struts. For a second longer I stared at him, and what they'd said about the Light Brigade at Balaclava came into my mind. I'd heard it repeated more than once in France, on one occasion by a bitter-mouthed brigadier whose infantry had been set some impossible task and been destroyed trying to achieve it. 'They want butchers not brigadiers,' he'd snarled. 'It might be magnificent, but it's never war.'

Neither was this.

As I slammed the pan of ammunition into place, I yanked the Lewis round and squinted down the sights. For a second, I couldn't make myself pull the trigger, because Guzmán looked so magnificent – a symbol of the old South-West, the old Medieval Mexico rushing to do battle with the aeroplane, that symbol of Twentieth-Century America.

As the gun clattered he seemed to stiffen in the saddle, then the arm that was holding his rifle up in the air slowly drooped, and he sagged forward to slip out of the saddle just as the horse crashed to the ground, sliding forward in the dust with its own tremendous momentum in a flurry of kicking legs. As the rumble of wheels beneath us stopped and the

DH lifted into the air, I saw them both sprawled on the ground and Villa's Dorados running towards them across the plateau. Suddenly, oddly, I felt sorry for what I'd done.

The landing strip was growing smaller now behind us as the DH lifted higher, lining up to the right and behind the Avro, and I could see the letters we'd built out of stones and the drifting smoke from the fire – Slingsby's 'RAF, Mexico'. I stared down at Villa's men round the fallen horse and rider, wondering what had really made him do it, then suddenly I became aware of my own tiredness. I glanced across at the Avro and saw that Puddy and Tommy were making signs of triumph to each other, but I also noticed that Slingsby's head had disappeared inside the rear cockpit and guessed that he'd settled down for a sleep, unable to keep his eyes open any longer.

Letting the gun, to which I was still clinging, fall back, I sank to the bottom of the cockpit. My eyes were already closing when I remembered that you didn't leave guns cocked. It was instinctive and I'd no more have thought of doing that than flying to the moon. Automatically, I took off the pan of ammunition, and put the safety catch on, then I sank back to the throbbing floor of the aeroplane again, still clutching the pan to my chest.

'Thank the Lord for aeroplanes,' I said aloud.

–

I was actually asleep when we rumbled to a stop at Camarillo. Vaguely I was aware of people helping me out and Charley flinging her arms round me and bursting into tears again: there was blood on my face and she clearly thought I was dying. Then I saw the Franklin, and as they pushed me into it I fell asleep again.

When I woke up I was in the hotel and the celebration that night was a corker. It seemed that the whole population of Camarillo was milling round, and those who weren't eating were yelling with excitement. Slingsby, looking as jaded as one of last year's autumn leaves, had his arm round Dominique Duellin, and I could see that Tommy was already struck by her and was trying to edge him away. Evalina, for her part, was clearly not intending to let Puddy get away again.

O'Hara was there with his lieutenant, and his men were all outside on the steps, drinking beer that had appeared from nowhere. Moat was there, too, smug and happy, because his story had gone out first – complete with the rescue by Villa. He was giving out titbits of information to two other reporters who'd arrived, but he was also making sure he kept all the best stories to himself. Dan Tucker's leathery face was creased in smiles and the Sheriff, probably under the influence of a bottle of 'mouthwash', was clearly not worrying about the laws of prohibition.

Then Ojarra arrived with his family and the place went mad, and Young Lukey, wild with the excitement of the occasion, rode his motor-bike up the wide front steps of the hotel and round the dining-room, scattering chairs and sending everyone on to table tops, yelling and laughing. It was the most tremendous celebration you could imagine because Guzmán was dead, and Camarillo felt safe. It seemed to go on all next day, too, as we gave joyrides in the aeroplanes to everybody who'd helped us – O'Hara, Young Lukey, the Sheriff. Even Old Lukey, who claimed the right for having given us a weather forecast, was levered into the rear cockpit of the Avro so he could claim to have done everything from riding a horse with Jeb Stuart's cavalry in 1864 to riding in 1920 in an Avro that had probably flown in France against the Germans.

'I'll tell ye a secret, son,' he murmured as I set him down. 'I was only sixteen and Stuart had already been killed when I joined his boys. But don't tell nobody.'

The next night was a more sober affair and, one arm round Charley, I sat on the front porch of the hotel in the dark. The newspapers had it that Villa was drawing near to Sabinas and, as far as I was concerned,

I hoped he won any battle that started. In fact, he did – with his very last *golpe terrifico* – and oddly enough three years later he, too, was dead, assassinated as he drove in retirement into town. Obregón followed him the same way five years later.

I looked across at Slingsby. It was quite clear the return journey to Europe would concern only two of the four of us who'd arrived together in the States. Busy with Dominique, Tommy was already home, and by the look on Evalina's face so was Puddy.

'What's going to happen now?' Slingsby asked.

'Back to the RAF, I suppose,' I said.

'It'll be a bit different from France and Russia.'

'Yes,' I agreed. 'More hard work. More what you'd call bread-and-butter flying, I suppose. There'll be a lot of that now we're supposed to be at peace. Are you staying in?'

'Actually—' Slingsby grinned '—I don't fancy bein' out. After all, they do look after you and, you never know, there might still be some fun.'